JOSEPH

The Father's Journey

MAC
McCONNELL

ONE WAY BOOKS

JOSEPH

Editor: Jodee Kulp, www.betterendings.org

ISBN 978-0-9800451-3-0   10 digit: 0-9800451-3-4
Library of Congress Catalog Card Number 2009907967

www.OneWayBookS.org — (954) 680-9095

APPRECIATION

Chapter two of this little book is inspired by a man whose life perfectly reflected Proverbs 22:1 – *"A good reputation is to be chosen above great riches."* I'm honored to have been numbered among his friends.
Gene A. Whiddon, Sr., 1928 – 1989

Fifteen years ago a man touched my life, and changed the course of my history that eventually led me to this page of this book and this chapter of my life. Thank you, Dr. Larry Thompson.

I owe a debt of gratitude to a friend that provides my oceanfront, writing getaway, each year. Your generosity is inspiring - your friendship a treasure. Thank you, Carl Kumpf.

I must continue to thank Linda, my bride of 30 + years, for her unbelievable patience, love and encouragement, especially during the intense months of editing these little volumes.

Thanks again to a very special lady and uncanny editor, Jodee Kulp. I never thought it possible to find someone that "gets" my writing. It is.

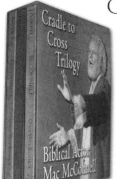

Cradle to Cross Trilogy

Joseph, Bozra and Hadad packaged together for the inside story of three eyewitnesses to the dangerous, romantic and traumatic times of 1st century Judae. The Cradle to Cross Trilogy will be an important addition to your favorites from Bible Actor Mac McConnell.

Cradle to Cross Trilogy Set
www.CradletoCrossTrilogy.org
Retail $29.95
9780980045161

"Joseph, I'm pregnant and the child isn't yours." The worst news any bridegroom could receive. Joseph is an unexpectant father now faced with decisions that effects all of history.

Joseph, The Father's Journey
5 x 7 Hard Cover - 128 pages
Retail $12.95
9780980045130

A shepherd misses the announcement of a lifetime. Angels tell of the birth of Messiah in Bethlehem. But Bozra is asleep on the job. His journey begins, though time after time he's a day late, until ...

Bozra, The Shepherd's Journey
5 x 7 Hard Cover - 128 pages
Retail $12.95
9780980045109

An innkeeper in Bethlehem blows it when the most famous guest in all of history is born under his nose. Hadad has customers, and no time for this dusty traveler, worn out donkey and very pregnant woman.

Hadad, The Innkeeper's Journey
5 x 7 Hard Cover - 128 pages
Retail $12.95
9780980045123

What they say about Mac's Writing

"You can feel his Joy and dedication, McConnell achieves a remarkable fluidity that moves this great historical novel until the receptive viewer becomes involved in its sincerity."

Bill van Maurer, critic, Miami Herald

"Mr. McConnell has expanded an already vivid character and introduced the reader to intimate details of culture and history."

K. Michaels

"As a student of the Bible myself, I was immediately intrigued by this wonderful book. It is a very easy read with a unique writing style and a HUGE message. I can hardly wait for the rest of the series!"

Tracy Kiesling

"Here is a great read, causes the reader to think and leaves the reader excitedly waiting for more of Mac McConnell's books."

Victoria Rose

"Mac places us in the bodies and minds of rich characters that lifts us out of the modern busy world and with few words gives us pages of crisp and stirring language."

Jodee Kulp

"I felt the rays of sun on my face, the mist in the air, the sand under my sandals, missed opportunities and then … Bozra is a wonderfully written story. I felt as though I was living and experiencing every facet of Bozra's life."

Debbie Kip

TABLE OF CONTENTS

Foreword

1.	Anytime	9
2.	Good Reputation	14
3.	She Asked About Me	22
4.	A Real Man	26
5.	A Better Idea	31
6.	Bitter Wine	41
7.	The Decision	46
8.	Secrets	54
9.	Three Pieces	68
10.	What Does This Mean?	74
11.	Five Days - Five Months	77
12.	The Stable	84
13.	The Innkeeper	92
14.	The Covenant	97
15.	The Dedication	102
16.	Proud Papa	114
17.	The Visit	119
18.	The Flight	124

Order Information

FOREWORD

Joseph was not a carpenter in our sense of the word, because houses were built mostly of stone and earth 2000 years ago. He was a woodworker or artist really, using wood, crafting furniture and innovative agricultural tools.

Joseph is an enchanting read full of how it could have been, facing challenges we may not be able to imagine, but quite possibly how you are or could be with Joseph's circumstances and his son right now.

Mac is not a writer in our sense of the word, because novels are often hundreds of pages which take weeks to read and often to places we would not care to go. He is an author or artist really, crafting with words that invoke many pages of innovative thoughts. Thoughts that we can sit on, that we can dig with, and that we can furrow out who we really are through these imaginative tales.

Chaplain Brian Doyle,
co-MVP New York Yankees
World Series 1978

ONE
Anytime

"Joseph, I'm all right. Don't worry, my husband, I'll be home soon. Joseph, I have wonderful news. My soul glorifies the Lord, and my spirit rejoices in God my Savior. I love you, Mary."

Just a flimsy scrap of parchment.
> Frayed, stained,
>> and wrinkled from the long journey.
>>> A short message.
>>> Short, and much too mysterious.

How could I be sure this was from Mary, my Mary? The fact that it is in my hands in the first place is a wonder.

Elias, my friend the butcher, said a man with a small company of travelers headed from Hebron all the way to Cana, asked him if he knew me, and said to be sure I receive this, this message.
> This pitiful excuse for an excuse.

It's been two long months with every day wondering what in the world is going on.

The whole town thinks they have to come by
and ask me,
    "Joseph, have you heard from Mary?"
      "Joseph, where did she go?"
        "Joseph, when will she return?"
          "Joseph, is the wedding still on?"

It's not enough for me to wonder *if* the wedding is still on.
    I'm reminded every day. If only I had a parrot to answer
    them, then maybe they would feel as stupid as me.
When I scream at my neighbors, "I DO NOT KNOW," they
    surely think I'm possessed. That might be my only
    excuse. This little girl. This little temptress. This little
    angel. This little creature that vanished into the desert
    with my heart might as well have cut it out and taken
    it with her.

I knew it was a mistake the first time I thought about her
    that way. She's too young. Too young for me I knew. I
    watched her grow up. I knew her family. Everyone did.
    Good people and good customers at that.
But, one day she ran right through my shed to play with my
    new pup—that cur that I needed like I needed another
    dull saw. Just seeing her play with my mutt was a joy
    and reason enough to keep him.
"What's his name?" Mary asked, scruffing his fur.
"I just call him, dog."

"That's silly. You should name him, umm, Jonah. Yes, Jonah."

"Jonah?"

"Mary," her father said, "Maybe naming his dog is Joseph's
decision, not yours."

"Jonah ... It's perfect," I said to my surprise.

Heli, her father, was a stiff fellow, stilted. A gangly man, slow
of speech and step. Had a way of crossing his arms before
he spoke. I thought a bit pious for these parts, but I was
wrong. Soon he came round often. Said he could appreciate an unwed man's life. No doubt he needed some
time away, with a wife, two daughters in the house, and
another child soon.

When Lois, his wife, asked me to join them for a meal
after temple, I tried to be polite and refuse, but Mary
surprised me.

"Joseph, you know you don't have another invitation." She
was right, but why did she care?

Then she disappeared with hardly a word. Not that she
should say anything to me, or be concerned with my
feelings. I was just enjoying her company round the table,
that's all.

But, she's just a child.

My friend's youngest daughter.

Mary's sister, on the other hand, had plenty to say. Lisha was
three full years older, "I'm not courting at the moment,"
she brought up in conversation more than once.

She's not hard on the eyes, but she can't hold a candle to
   Mary. Not that that was important to me. Lisha said
   something about helping her with their barn door as I
   left. My mind was elsewhere, perhaps wondering what
   happened to Mary all of a sudden, and I said, "Anytime."
      Anytime was apparently the next day.

"Joseph." A familiar voice interrupted my work. "If you
   come now to look at that door, you'll be just in time for
   the noon meal." It was Lisha, the sister.
"Door? What door?" I said abruptly, wiping sweat from my
   brow. She looked hurt.
"Th—the barn door I mentioned yesterday." She turned to
   leave.
"Oh, yes, of course. That door. Now will be fine." It wasn't,
   but I felt guilty, and more than a little hungry.
Maybe Mary was there. I didn't ask.

Mary was not there.
   No one was.
And the door barely needed any attention at all.
Lisha was overly attentive, and overly dressed for midday.
   And she had an opinion about everything.
"Don't you think Nazareth is a good place to raise a family,
   Joseph?"
"A family? Yes, I believe so." *What do I know about family?*
"Don't you think a mature woman makes a good wife,
   Joseph?"

Anytime

"Mature? Wife? I, I don't know about that." *What am I supposed to know about wives?*

"Joseph, you are so strong. Is that because you're a carpenter? I'll bet that's it." She squeezed my arm.

Her eyes were dancing.

"Oh my goodness, I have so much work to do."

I got up, wiped my mouth, and started to leave.

"Do you have to leave so soon? No one will be back for hours, Joseph."

Was she …?

I think she was.

"Yes, I do. Thanks for lunch and all, and please give my regards to Mary." As I crossed the threshold I heard her say, *'Mary'* between her teeth.

It wasn't long till all I thought about was Mary.

And I had to wonder what a lovely girl like Mary would see in me. But if I don't marry soon, well, the choices were diminishing by the day.

I had had inquiries.

Father had had inquiries,

but Mary was only the second girl I had ever been interested in, and the thought of having a family, well, the first girl's family didn't approve of "just a carpenter."

I never told *her* how I felt.

She married a lawyer.

TWO
Good Reputation

Nazareth was never much of a town till of late. Many used to head south to Nain, Scythopolis, or north to find work near Dalmanutha or even Capernaum, never to return. But trade routes are changing. Romans setting in at Port Ptolemais and traveling down the coast or straight over to Bethsaida, or Tiberias. My little business is very good, if not demanding. That may very well be due to my father's lesson one day. I was his apprentice, which often felt more like being a slave.

But it was a lesson that stuck,
  that changed my life, at least my attitude.
   That started with a simple question,
    so, I thought.
"Father," I asked. "Why are we so backed up with orders?"
  I knew we were the only real carpenters in Nazareth. I also knew we received work from Cana and Magdala and more than once from Caesarea on the coast. But Father never rushed me with my work. I learned it was

not finished till I could say *yes* to his favorite question,
"Is that the best you can do?"

Too many times, I would go back and see, it was not my best.

"You can do better, son. I don't want to see your face until
it's your best."

Sometimes *my* best was not *his* best. Then he showed
me, and sent me back for a rework.

Humiliating, but the reward of Father's approval
made me forget those times.

"Son," Father said. "Why are we backed up? I have a question for you. Who was the wisest man who ever lived?"

"Why, Solomon, King Solomon, Father? He was the wisest
man who ever lived." I grinned with that answer on
the tip on my tongue. Father liked it when I knew the
answer. Or maybe, he's just hoping my schooling wasn't
wasted.

"And son, who was the richest man who ever lived?" Father
thought he might trick me.

"Father, that was King Solomon too." I looked for his reac-
tion.

"Well now, if the wisest man who ever lived, and the richest
man who ever lived, had something to say about business, should we listen?"

"Yes, of course. Is this a trick question?" I was laughing a
little and took a seat. I knew Father was about to instruct,
and expected complete attention.

"Son, King Solomon said, 'A good reputation is to be chosen above great riches.'"

"Yes, but we are doing good. You never complain about our savings. We have a good reputation. We have lots of work, maybe too much."

I forget to keep my mouth shut sometimes.

Father prefers me to listen and not act too smart for my own good. He said more than once, "How are you going to learn with your mouth flapping?"

"All that is true, son, but it wasn't always that way."

"Father, is there something wrong with having money?" I thought this was a good question.

"What did Solomon say about riches?"

"That, that a reputation is more important?" My mouth was sinking me deeper.

"Close, my son. Sometimes it's good to see what he *didn't* say."

I looked curious for Father's benefit.

"See, Solomon didn't say, a good reputation is to be chosen *instead* of great riches."

"Yes, but ... " This was getting tedious.

"No buts. Just listen. Solomon said a reputation is to be chosen."

"So, if we have a choice, we should choose a good reputation." I blurted and regretted. But not for long.

"Perfect," he said.

I got a *perfect*. "But ... "

"Could you just listen?"

"Yes, sir." I dropped my head. I had good ideas too, but Father preferred to be the authority.

"We were not always successful, Joseph. There was a time your mother had to take in laundry and mend clothes for the wealthy. There were times I worked for someone else to get by. There was a time I had debt on our little house. There was a time I had to buy wood on credit not knowing when, or if, I could pay them back. There was a time ... " Father was actually getting flustered. His face, his cheeks, were flushed.

"Son, I thought I was a failure."

"But, Father, that must have been a long time ago. You are the most respected man in the city." This was the first time I'd seen my rough old father show signs of weakness and I wanted to stop it—to encourage him.

"Yes, a long time ago, but the memory serves to remind me of who I am and where I came from."

Father was a proud man and I was surprised to hear this side of him. He was a big man, and tough as nails. Not always a kind man, and disappointed with anyone who did not carry their own weight. He was often impatient with my pitiful work ethic. It was really my daydreaming that infuriated him.

I couldn't help it, my mind just loved to wonder—to wander. I love to think, what if?

"Where was I, Joseph?"

"You said, perfect. I said, we should choose a good reputation. And you said perfect." I was glad to remind him.

"Yes, choose. Right answer. It is a matter of choice. I learned it the hard way, but I learned it and you will too, my son, or just be skimping along in life." Confident and determined, Father was back. I was relieved.

"Here's the point."

"Finally," I mumbled.

"I heard that." But he was smiling. He began to pace.

"When reading my scroll one day—the Proverbs—I read 'a good reputation is to be chosen above great riches.' I thought about that. I had always been trying to make a good living. Better than good, I wanted to be well off, but always seemed to be behind, struggling. I thought, if Solomon says a good reputation, a good name, is more important to him, then it should be more important to me." Father was all wound up and I must admit, I was captivated.

"Joseph, you're a good boy, I should say, a fine young man, but that's not enough. You must think about being your best. Then, and only then, will you have a reputation that will carry you through tough times."

"Have I known tough times, Father?"

"No, that's because of your mother and me, and that's the way we want it. But, we can't shelter you forever. You will have trials you could never expect. We want you to value things that last. Now think about that. Your reputation, your name, right now, is tied to mine."

I had never thought about it that way.

"The time will come when you will make a name for your-self—good or bad. Building a good name takes time. And it can be destroyed," Father snapped his finger in my face, "Just like that." He sat down on the bench, and looked me straight in my eyes.

"Son, I had to change, to choose to change my whole idea of making a living. I had to stop trying to make a living altogether."

"Father, that makes no sense."

"At least you are paying attention. Now here's the point."

I wanted to say, *You said that already*. But I held back.

"I told your mother, starting at that moment, I am concen-trating on one thing, and that one thing is making a repu-tation for being the best carpenter in Nazareth, maybe all of Galilee. She said, 'all of Nazareth will certainly do, Jacob,' but, Joseph I had bigger dreams."

I don't know what I was more excited about, Father's enthu-siasm, or that he was a dreamer too.

"Father, I think you did that. How? What did you do? Father, this is the most excited I have ever seen you."

"Well, except when I met your mother."

"Father, one thing at a time, please." That made him laugh right out loud. I was thrilled I made my father laugh so hard. "What did you do? How did you start?"

"Both good questions, Joseph. First I had to think, I have a pretty good reputation for being a pretty good carpenter. But, I had to admit, no one said I was the best. I had to take stock and admit that sometimes I cut corners, or charged more than I should, if I thought my customer could afford it."

I was surprised again.

"But that must have changed, Father. Everyone says you are the best." I thought about saying that not everyone says he is the most tactful, but I didn't. Father could be impatient. If someone questioned something, he'd snap back, "You aren't listening, are you?"

"That did not happen overnight, Joseph. Here's what I did. First I walked out to the shed and looked at the table due for delivery. I thought it was done, finished. But the more I looked, I knew I could do better. I hoisted it back on my work bench and began sanding. I sharpened my plane and took the table down a bit more. I sanded more. When I thought it was just so, I took olive oil, mixed with linseed and wiped it down. The more I studied it, the more pleased I was and the more I polished. The grain had a bright sheen, the knots glistened in the beauty of the wood. I was proud."

"When my customer came to pick it up, he looked right past it and said, 'Jacob, I thought you said my table was ready.' I said, 'Yes, you almost tripped over it.' 'This is my table? It's beautiful. That can't be mine. I can't afford such a fine table. Jacob, really where is mine? he said.'

"It took some convincing, but finally he took it, shaking his head and thanking me. He said, 'Jacob, this is the best table I have ever seen.' And, Joseph, it was worth it. To hear him say that, made it worth it. I was sure I'd made the right choice as he sent me a referral the very next day. Since then everything I do is the best I can do. And everyone knows that Jacob does the best work and charges a fair price.

"Joseph, we are not expensive, but too good to be cheap. And listen, this is great. Since that day I have never had a time when we could not pay our bills. Soon we were out of debt and now have savings set aside for most emergencies, and never fail to tithe."

Father told me more. And I decided if it was that important to him, I would make it important to me.

I decided his reputation would be safe with me, and I would teach my son the importance of guarding *his* father's reputation too.

THREE
She Asked About Me

Heli came the day after my little adventure with Lisha. Mary was with him.

"Joseph, I want to thank you for tending to my door. What do I owe you?"

"Owe me? Not a thing. It was nothing, and I did have a meal."

"Oh, is that right? I trust Lisha treated you well."

He looked surprised. I suspected he didn't appreciate me being alone with her.

"Joseph, do you have intentions for my daughter?" I was not ready for that question. Did he mean Lisha or Mary? Mary squinted her eyes at her father.

"Sir, I simply adjusted the door. Had a little meal and left. That's all." Mary looked relieved. Could she possibly have an interest in the likes of me?

"All right then, I didn't mean to sound so ... I apologize." He was sincere, but I couldn't help but think, any intentions I have for Mary could easily be a waste of time.

In fact, what was I thinking? Mary's a child.

She Asked About Me

Little more than a child.
A beautiful child, but a child.
I wanted to ask how old she is,
      but was sure that would be rude, or worse.

"If you won't let me compensate you, then please, come
    round for a Shabbat dinner with the whole family."
      I thought *that* could be awkward.
"Father, could I stay and play a bit with Jonah?" Mary said.
    This *was* awkward.
"No, Mary. Your mother expects your help with the ... the
    housework." I was glad he came up with something.
    I was sure I would do or say something stupid. She
    frowned again. She glanced at me. Just a little glance.
But it sure looked promising.
    I was in big trouble.

I couldn't help but think of my father's excitement that day,
    "Well son, except when I met your mother." I may be
    more confused than excited. I couldn't tell the difference.

"Joseph." It was Phinehas, my friend and best customer of
    late. In a hurry as usual. "Is my cupboard ready?"
"I, I will have to see. Why don't you come take a look."
"You don't know if it's ready?"
    I wasn't sure I knew anything at that moment.

"Just come and give me your opinion. I want to make sure you're pleased."

"I never worry about that. Your work is the best, Joseph. By the way, you know my cousin. She would like it very much if you could come to dinner someday. What do you say? She seems interested in you."

"Oh, I don't know, I don't think I'm ready to settle down just yet."

"You are not getting any younger, Joseph. And the way you were enjoying the festivities at the Feast, well, you were the talk of the town."

I was afraid of that. I had a little too much wine, and the food, and the music, and the dancing, and oh, the headache the next morning. I wondered ...,

"Phinehas, did I make a fool out of myself?" I really didn't want to know.

"Let's put it this way. It's obvious you knew how to have a good time. And many were delighted to see you enjoy yourself instead of buried behind wood chips and sawdust."

I think that was good news.

"And, Joseph, where'd you learn to sing like that?"

"Oh, don't tell me. I didn't, did I?"

"Yes, and very impressive. Were you leading the Israelites across the Red Sea?" Phinehas was laughing too hard for my liking.

"Just tell me if the cupboard meets your approval, and we can call it a day." I wanted to change the subject.

"Joseph, it's beautiful as always. And, Joseph, I need a crib. And soon."

"From me."

"Yes. You know the wife is expecting, and the time is close."

"And you know I will have to charge you too much. Anyone can make you a crib. Why don't you borrow one?"

"I thought about that, Joseph, but this is our first and wifey said she wanted a brand new one made by Joseph, the carpenter. I think that's you."

"Well, then, whatever you say. Come, let's pick the wood."

"You pick, Joseph. I trust you."

"All right, but don't complain about the price."

"And, Joseph, was that Heli and Mary who just left? Do you think Mary would be a help to my wife when the baby comes?"

Mary? I can't get a moment's relief. "How should I know?"

"Sorry, I thought, never mind then. Wifey said she asked about you yesterday."

"No she didn't. Have you forgotten, *thou shalt not lie*."

"Have it your way. I'll be back for my cupboard, and thanks for taking on the crib. We wouldn't have it any other way."

Mary asked about me.

FOUR
A Real Man

Phinehas had his baby, that is, his wife did.
"Joseph, I have a son. We named him after you."
"You did? I am honored." I really was.
"No, not really. But we considered it at least."
"You are so funny. I hope you are proud of yourself."

He was proud, of course, with a brand new son. And I was
happy for them. And thought about the day I might
have a son. I *would* name my son after me. Joseph, my
son. Joseph junior. I could tell everyone I named him
Joseph after the most famous Joseph, son of Jacob, who
was exiled and became the savior of the Israelite people
in Egypt. That may be presumptuous. Thinking I could
have a son of such stature. The patriarch, Jacob, was
Joseph's father. Jacob ... my father's name.

Gave me chills.

What must it be like to have a son
who saves his people?

Real Man

Now, the Romans are taking up where the Egyptians left off. They are slowly, but surely, moving in, establishing control, imposing restrictions and new taxes. Nazareth had missed most of it, but travelers brought frightening news of terror, torture and crucifixions to rebels. Most Romans, not all I hope, despise Jew's. Who knows why?

A few of us began to train secretly with swords and spears and daggers. I fashioned some weapons with wood and chains and iron. One, a scythe, I shortened and added a strap. I was surprised this idea came so readily.

Jamlech, a neighbor, helped train us. He'd spent a year at Tyre, a substantial Roman garrison. "They trained every-day, and then got drunk each night." He told us.

"Is that last part a requirement?" I asked.

None of us hoped for any real confrontation, and certainly not any kind of battle, but we agreed, to do nothing was no longer an option. My work kept me in good condition. Better than most, I must say. However, I wasn't looking for bloodshed. I wondered if I'd make much of a soldier. But there was something in me that I knew would protect the innocent. And to think, if Mary was in trouble, and I did not, or could not protect her, well, that was all the motivation I needed.

I was shocked at how stimulated I was. I wanted to be known as a man after God's heart, not a warrior.

"Joseph, easy now, this is just training. Just practice."
Jamlech was a good teacher, but out of breath, and looked
a little concerned about my fervor for the fight.
This was quite a contrast. At one time I considered going
on with my studies. Seeking a mentor, a rabbi to teach
me. Nazareth has a large synagogue and a priest in
residence. Torah fascinated me. The stories, the battles,
the words, leapt off the page. Our rabbi allowed me to
slip into temple, open the scrolls and read them aloud.
I pretended to be the priest, the temple filled with all in
awe of my knowledge. But Father insisted being Jewish
meant family business. His father was a carpenter. And
his father's father before him. I would be a carpenter and
my son would be a carpenter, he said.
"Joseph, becoming a priest is an honorable desire, do not
misunderstand me. But, you my son, have a gift, a love
for wood and tools, and are better than I with customers. I will not forbid you if God has spoken to you about
this. However, if being a priest is your desire and not
Jehovah's, you will become a sham, live a lie, and do
more harm than good. I assure you, Joseph, God has a
plan just for you. A perfect plan."

Father was so sure of what he was saying that I had perfect
peace. I can't explain it, but I was as certain as Father.
That day, my love for woodworking became as important,
as necessary to me, as anything I'd known. It was as if
my tools were an extension of my arms. As if the wood

I was working had life. I wanted to do my best. Not just because of the wrath of Father, but I wanted to honor God with the talent he gave me.

Soon I surprised Father, and myself, for that matter. I would barely finish breakfast and head for the shed. I had a longing, a compulsion, to see my latest project. To run my hands along the grain. To see God's creation in my work. I no longer *wanted* to do my best. I *needed* to do my best. I would not settle for less. I felt pride in my work, myself. But different, with confidence that didn't need to boast. Father approved as I selected just the right piece of timber for a project.

Our supplier, Dekar, wanted to do business with Father, not me. And always in a hurry.

"Jacob, your son takes too long. He's so fussy. It's just wood."

"Just wood? Just wood? Would you say that mountain is just a mountain? That lake is just a lake? A sunrise is just a sunrise? Don't you see the wonder in wood? Joseph, my son, is *fussy* because he wants only the best. You should be proud he does business with you. Who's your best customer, Dekar? You are not the only woodman in town."

Father was adamant. And I, more proud that day than I can remember to be his son.

"Take your time, son," Father said while staring at Dekar. Daring him to disagree.

"Yes. By all means. Take your time, Joseph. You should take all the time you need." Dekar actually sounded sincere.

I took my time.

"Perhaps you should cull your load before you come dragging by here the next time," Father said as he counted out the coins and handed them to the man.

"Good idea, Jacob. I will do just that."

"Joseph, my son, I think you could show me a thing or two. You've passed me by with your skill and determination."

"Never, Father, you're still the best." I was not being completely truthful.

"The fact is son, I wouldn't have it any other way. A son should go from student to teacher. The best compliment I receive is when someone says, 'Could you have Joseph do this one for me, Jacob?' And I know I have taught you all I could."

At dinner that night I was a bit full of myself. Beaming a bit, I'm sure. Mother placed a bowl of olives and grape leaves on the table. I mumbled, "Is that the best you can do?"

Father snatched my arm and me to my feet. "Joseph, how dare you speak to your mother like that." Mother gasped.

"Apologize. Now!"

I did, and knew,

I had more to learn about being a real man.

FIVE
A Better Idea

My love, no my romance of wood and work grew.

Father and I would discuss Proverbs amidst sawdust hanging in the air. I was amazed at his memory and precise interpretation of Torah. It rubbed off on me. Day after day we worked side by side talking and discussing, or saying nothing at all.

I asked one night at dinner, "Is it proper that I should not want to marry? To devote myself to work? And to God, of course."

"So, you want to break your mother's heart?" Mother did look heartbroken. "And rob your mother of the most precious gift of a grandchild?" She added immediately.

"Joseph, who will you train? Who will carry on our line, our name?" Father joined the attack. "I saw how you looked at that pretty little thing, Lelah, when she and her father came to see our progress on their mantel. You really think you can deny your feelings? You are a man Joseph, some things are meant to be."

"And, Joseph, you want your mother to go to her grave without the joy of holding your first born? How could you say such a thing?" Mother was staring at me. Her mouth quivered.

"And Joseph, I'm not getting any younger. You will need help. You should have your own son in the business. This is the heart's desire of any father."

"Apparently, you two don't think this was a good idea," I said.

"A terrible idea," they said at once, nodding, lips tight.

It wasn't long until I thought, *how indulgent*?

To think I could be satisfied being alone.

There is only so much a piece of wood can do.

Some of our customers brought their daughters to have a look at me, and me to have a look at them. Father encouraged them. I was interested from time to time, but felt like I was cheating on my work. That I was contemplating a mistress instead of my first love.

Until that little child.

That little girl.

That Mary.

Thoughts of her made me dream a better dream.

The day my son was working beside me.

I would teach him the things of God.

A Better Idea

My mind was mush when Mary showed up with her father. But now this. As much as I loved my woodworking, it never affected me like this! I read the thing again.

"Joseph, I'm all right. Don't worry, my husband, I'll be home soon. Joseph, I have wonderful news. My soul glorifies the Lord, and my spirit rejoices in God my Savior. I love you, Mary."

I was relieved to get her note. But I needed to understand why she left like that in the first place. We were spending so much time together that there was talk in the town. Heli would show up unexpected and scold us both. Father was not happy about the gossip. I was happy to have work to do—to keep my sanity. Her sister finally became engaged and we were able to court openly. Still, there was gossip about our ages, but even Heli finally conceded since there was nothing he could do. He and Father made the arrangements without bothering to tell me. There wasn't much to arrange.

I knew I loved her.

I knew she loved me.

I thought she loved me.

We were inseparable. Could hardly take our eyes off of each other. I could not stand it any longer.

Mary finally had her birthday.

She was now considered a woman beginning her fourteenth
year. I in my twentieth. Mother and Father warned me
that our age difference, our levels of maturity, could
make things difficult.

Mary simply said, "Joseph, I am a woman."

"I understand, Mary."

I did understand.

Mostly.

And mostly, did not want her to explain further.

Then … then she left without a word.

It seemed childish and inconsistent, immature and disre-
spectful. I felt like an idiot when I went to see her.

"Oh, Joseph, good to see you," Lois greeted me, Heli behind
her.

"Yes, and good to see you. Where's Mary?"

"You, you don't know?" They looked at each other.

"Know what?"

"Heli, Lois, know what? Is, is Mary all right?" I had not
considered that something could ever happen to Mary.
That she could become ill or injured or anything.

"Joseph, she's gone to see, to spend some time with her
cousin Elizabeth in Juttah."

"Juttah? All the way to Hebron? I don't understand."

"We were sure she told you. We received word that Elizabeth
was with child."

"With child. Not her cousin, Elizabeth? She's … "

"Too old? That's what we thought, but we were wrong. And Mary was so excited she left immediately."

"Not by herself?"

"No, of course not. She joined her cousin Beri and his wife Zoe. They were on their way to Hebron. She had to hurry. I suppose that's why she missed telling you. Joseph, I'm sorry, but ... "

"When will she be back?"

"At least a month. It's three, maybe four days to Juttah, and Elizabeth and Zechariah are further still. Come, have some tea."

"No—some other time."

I must've looked pretty dumb. A blank look on my face, and an empty hole in my gut. Nauseous.

Mary just upped and left? A month? We could barely spend the day apart and now she is going to be gone a month. Is she having second thoughts?

Am I?

She was close to Elizabeth, I knew. I'm sure when she heard that her cousin was going to have a child, she couldn't wait to see her. She had a special love for babies. When Phinehas had theirs, Mary was there every day. She would bring the child to see me, a smile stretched across her face.

"Someday, Joseph."
I knew what she meant.
    I blushed, but only a little.

If it wasn't for her note, what would I think?
What does *soon* really mean.
This being in love can drive a man out of his mind.

I kept myself busy. But nothing I did was right.
Father told me to take some time off. He said everything I
    touched I made worse.

Now, I haven't mentioned that we became formally betrothed.
A traumatic experience.
When her sister was finally promised, I knew I shouldn't
    wait any longer, but Father said, "Don't be so anxious,
    keep your self-respect."
I was pretty sure my self-respect had lost its self-respect.
    I wasn't sure who to ask first. Mary or her father.
I thought I'd better make things certain with Mary, then leave
    the details to Father and Heli.

We were just going for a walk.
Every time I opened my mouth it was dry as dust.
I tried to say something several times. It was really simple,
    but kept getting stuck in my throat.

"Joseph, something on your mind?"

"Mary?"

"I'm listening."

"Mary, let's have a family."

"Joseph, should we have a wedding first?"

   We laughed.

"Yes, that's a good idea, Mary. Will you … "

"Yes!" She pounded my arm. "What took you so long?"

That was a good question.

"You must ask Father."

"I know, Mary."

"When?"

"Mary, I will ask him soon."

"Real soon." It was a declaration. "Joseph, I don't know how
   I could possibly wait the whole year of betrothal to be
   with you. To start a family." She moved in close.

Now I was really nervous.

"It's about time, my son." Father had hinted and hinted,
   and Mother, oh my, could not see me for a minute without prodding me. They got over our age differences. I
   thought it would have been nice if they told me.

"Can we go now?" I had made up my mind and didn't want
   to change it. What if Heli says no? The business of
   betrothal can be complicated with the fathers of some

girls, handsome girls that is. We would have to agree on the shilukin, the dowry, agree on the date, agree on who would chaperone.

I wanted to tell Mary we should just sneak off and be done with it, but I knew better.

"Heli, I'm going to marry, Mary."

"Is that so? Who told you you could marry, Mary?" I just stared at Heli. Our relationship was not the biggest secret in town. What was this all about?

"Joseph, I asked you a question."

"I don't understand, Heli. You are against our marriage?"

"You must ask properly, Joseph."

"Yes, of course. I was just a little, you know. Heli, father of my love, I am asking for your permission to betroth your daughter … "

"Joseph, perhaps I could be of some assistance."

Father! I had forgotten, this is the Father's business, the Shiddukhin, the matchmaker. They both let it loose at once. Laughing. At me.

I deserved it.

"Heli, Joseph's mother and I wish to seek an arrangement for the betrothal of Joseph and your lovely daughter, Mary."

"That's *some* better. I will have to think about that … of course, you have my permission. We have agreed on the dowry and we will sanction the match."

They had agreed on the dowry?

So, this was a complete set-up?

A Better Idea

I didn't know which one I wanted to strangle first.

"But, know this, Joseph, this is my daughter, and she deserves your very best."

I agreed, and as I took my leave, *I am going to marry, Mary* was still on my lips. And then it began to sink in, *I am going to marry, Mary*. I am going to marry this beautiful little angel. Joseph, *you are the most fortunate man in Judea*. God is more than merciful, he is ... I have found his favor.

I have received God's gift of the most wonderful hope, to have Mary as my bride.

The mother of my children.

The betrothal would be for a year.

No, for an eternity.

We were already ready. "Oh, but tradition says—there will be such talk." I am reminded by everyone, but not, Mary.

"Mary, why would you want to marry me?" I was asking for disappointment here.

"I love you, Joseph. I prayed to God to provide for me the perfect husband. For a man after God's heart and God's pleasure. I asked God to give me a deep love for a man who loved his word. I didn't ask for a handsome man. I didn't ask for a strong man, or for a successful man or a man of respect and character."

"You didn't?"

"No, I didn't have to. You already are those things.
And what did you pray for, my husband?"

I wanted to tell her something as extraordinary as she said
to me. But I had this habit of telling the truth, often to
my own embarrassment—like now. What could I tell
her? What would I tell her? What?

"Joseph … ?"

"Mary, I must tell you the truth. From the moment I saw
you I just prayed God would give you a love for me, for
I was suddenly hopelessly in love with you. I knew there
was nothing I could do to deserve you, so God was just
going to have to do it. To put it on your heart."

"So I should blame God then?"

"Mary!"

"Oh, Joseph, I'm just having some fun with you."

"Mary, how can we possibly wait for an entire year?"

"Joseph, you know your parents and mine will insist we follow tradition. We must pray for God to provide a way."

"Then, Mary, can we blame God when we marry before the
year is out?"

"Joseph!"

SIX
Bitter Wine

But now this. I'm supposed to hold on to this scrap of a note?
   This is the hope I have?
If I knew that this little girl was going to tear at my heart,
   keep me awake all night,
      to make me do and say dim-witted things,
         well, I just don't know.

I started work on our new home. Father insisted I take the
   acreage north, up the hill a bit, that had been in our family for years. It didn't take much convincing—you should
   see this property. The view, the woods, the meadow. We
   worked on our orders and projects till mid-afternoon,
   then up to the house. A modest beginning, but much
   more than most. Mary and me would not have to impose
   on either of our families.
      I was grateful.
"Father, I am beside myself with Mary. She just up and left.
   All I have is this note she sent."

"What does it say?" I read it to Father. I didn't need to read it at all. It was seared into my brain.

"I can't but wonder, Father, if she is having second thoughts? She seems so mature, but this, so childish. To run off like that without so much as a word."

"Son, she said she has wonderful news."

"I know, but what could be so wonderful that she had to leave, or that she couldn't explain in the note she sent?"

"Maybe she has found a way to move the wedding up."

"Father, that *would* be wonderful news."

I had hope again.

I had a smile again.

I had confidence again.

Father was surely right. That was the only explanation. What wonderful news that would be.

Folks still ask, "When will Mary be back?" But now I could say with confidence, "Soon, and we will share some wonderful news."

One month slipped into two. Two became three.

Her note began to fade with my hope and excuses to the many questions.

Our house was nearly finished, and I wondered if we would ever use it. Would she ever come home?

Her *soon* was becoming ridiculous. My mood was too. I had no choice but to wait and wonder.

Bitter Wine

I hated to show my face in public.
Going to temple was difficult, but I did my best to appear
optimistic.

I moved into our house, alone.
    I hoped it would be *our* house. Then every night at twi-
light, just to satisfy myself, I looked down the road. The
view was breathtaking from the side of our little hill. I
could see right past Heli's cottage to the road south.
I could see anyone on that road as the sun set,
    but I wasn't looking for just anyone.

It happened. I had to pinch myself.
It was just a girl on a donkey, a silhouette is all.
But there was something …
    I could tell it was my Mary, but wondered if I was
dreaming—just wishful thinking. It had been over three
months since I laid eyes on her.
      I wondered if they were playing tricks on me.
No, she was unmistakable.
I started down the path, slowly.
    Should I go to her?
    Does she want to see me?
    Have things changed?
    Was I the fool?
The hurt and worry were deep.

She passed by her home. She was coming up the hill.
Towards me.
This is ridiculous.
I started. Cautious at first.
Then I picked up the pace. To run.
Mary. My beautiful Mary is home.
Just as I reached her, she began to slide off her mount into
    my arms.
A glow on her face
    she was radiant
        heavenly.
I wrapped my arms around my Mary—and—this can't be.

    Wait.
        What in the world?

I stepped back to see if what I felt, on her stomach against
    mine, in our embrace, was true.
But it was dusk and hard to see and her clothes were loose.

"Mary? What's this? Are you? You're not … "
"Yes, Joseph, yes, it's true. I told you I have wonderful news.
    You did receive my note?"
"Mary, you are preg …?"
    I thought I was going to throw up right there, right then.
    I turned to leave.

Bitter Wine

"Joseph, wait. I can explain. This *is* wonderful news. Wait. Listen to me. Don't leave. Can't you just wait for one minute? Joseph, it will be fine. Joseph … "

The sound of her voice was fading as I stomped off.

I didn't want to hear, '*This is wonderful news.*'

To hear, '*Listen to me.*'

I didn't want to hear anything at all.

'*I can explain,*' she said.

'*It will be fine,*' she said.

I tore through the door, and slammed it behind. It rattled the whole house and frightened Jonah. He came and reared up for his head-rub. I pushed him aside and continued out back and knocked a stool out of my way. I sat in the garden. The one I made for her. Then I tore it to pieces. Ripped the vines from the archway and slung them away. I kicked the flowers. Broke the pots. Grabbed the trellis to tear it to pieces, but crumbled to my knees. "Why, oh God, why?"

He didn't answer.

I now had an answer to, *is the wedding still on?*

I found my wine.

The wine bought special for our wedding night.

It tasted bitter.

Perfect.

SEVEN
The Decision

Jonah woke me, whining and licking my face.

I had passed out in our little courtyard. *My* courtyard. My neck was aching. There was dried blood on my hands and splinters in my fist. I raised up on one elbow to see the mess I made. It all came back to me. I looked to see if she was there. If she had any explanation for this treachery.

I decided the cleanup could wait,

I had other decisions to make.

It was clear.

Perfectly clear—I had the right—every right—to take her to court and prove that this girl is pregnant without my involvement.

I knew it could not be me. I had never touched her. Not in that way. We had not even thought about it—well, thought—but that's all. We couldn't help thinking about it. And Mary was so anxious to start a family, to have a baby of her own. She fussed over every baby in town.

The Decision

That is it, for god's sake. She wanted a baby so bad she
   couldn't wait till she came back home? I started to pack
   a few things and head to Juttah to find this fellow and
   slit his god-forsaken throat. Then I thought, it's a good
   thing he's so far away, I would have done it already.
   But of course I would have to prove it or be stoned for
   murder myself.
      Which at the moment was just fine with me.
The public humiliation would kill me anyway.
What about my reputation? I spent my whole life building
   my reputation as an honest and honorable man.
What will people think? That Mary is a harlot.
      That we couldn't wait? That I was responsible?
      That she had a secret lover all the time.
The gossips will have a time with this.

I expected Heli at any minute with the militia to run me out
   of town, or worse. How will it sound when I tell him,
   "It wasn't me"?
Mother and Father will be out of their minds.
      I know I was.

I washed my face and changed clothes.
      I needed to tell them.
      I needed advice.
They were already coming to see me.
      Had they heard?

"Joseph, son, are you all right?" Mother asked. "You look awful."

"Have you heard?"

"Heard? We heard Mary is home. Where is she?"

"What do I care?"

"Joseph, what in the world?" Father looked confused.

"She's pregnant."

"Joseph, who is pregnant?"

"You heard me. Mary is pregnant, and don't even look at me like that. Not by me."

The silence was stunning. A hard silence. They collapsed on the bench. Their heads sunk. Who knew what to say?

"Joseph, before you do anything, you need to talk to Heli and Mary and her mother."

"Talk? What is there to talk about?"

"Son, you will be sorry if you rush into anything. Things are not always as they seem."

"Is that right, Father? I may not be sophisticated as some, but I know this. Mary is pregnant. She did not even deny it. Soon she'll be showing. Everyone will know. Every one will be talking. My reputation is at stake here, Father."

Mother sobbed. She had never heard Father and I argue like this, and Father unable to calm me down.

"Son, let's go for a walk. Mother, we will be back." Father was in the habit of calling Mother *Mother* when he was serious.

"Father, I have no choice."

"You always have a choice, son. And, Joseph, you make good choices. The important thing is to make a choice you can live with. If Mary is pregnant … "

"No *if* about it, Father."

"Then, *since* Mary is pregnant, you must make the very best decision for everyone. For Mary, for you, for her parents, for us, for our community, for our faith, for God's sake. What would you decide then?"

"Father, have you thought for just a moment that this is your son speaking here? Have you thought for a moment what you would do if it were you? Have you thought, what if it was your bride?"

"Stop right there. Joseph, that's enough."

It wasn't enough for me. Father wasn't even sympathetic. He always took the other person's side. I needed a friend, not a father. The more he tried to calm me down the more convinced I became.

"Father, I should see Rabbi Mattaniah."

"Joseph, if you do that, it will be over. Perhaps you should just have a civil ceremony."

"What are you saying? Have you heard a word I said? This is not my child. Why would I marry her? Have you lost your mind?" Certainly I was having a nightmare.

"Just think about it," Father mumbled.

"Father, you don't believe me, do you? You want a grandson
so bad ... , and then you suggest a pagan ceremony? Am
I hearing you right?"

"Joseph, I know you're hurt and confused."

"Brilliant." If only I could just haul off and slug him.

"I know, I know, you are mad at me. I deserve that. Honestly,
I do not know what I'd do in your place. I don't want
to think about it."

"But, you want me to think about it?"

"Yes, I do. Very much. I'm asking you to think this through."

"That's what you would do?"

"No, probably not, but you are a better man than I, Joseph."
Finally a little consolation.

"I will make you a pact. Give this some time. Through the
Sabbath, and then, whatever you decide, I will back you
completely." Father's eyes were red and wet.

He hugged me and left,
    not waiting for an answer,
        leaving me no choice.

Forty-eight hours—another eternity.

I couldn't think straight.

I couldn't work.

I could barely stand the house. The house I built for my
little harlot.

The Decision

Was God just using this to humiliate me?
To smash my pride?

It was working.

I *had been* the happiest man in Nazareth.

Successful. Betrothed to an angel. The envy of every single
man in town, and a few married ones too.

Well, "Thanks God," this will take care of that.

I will be the laughingstock.

I dragged myself to temple on Shabbat. I could not begin to
tell you what the rabbi's message was, or the scripture
reading, for that matter. I was much too concerned with
what anyone might say or ask. But no one seemed the
least bit interested in me, for a change. Most had asked
over and over when Mary was coming home. It appeared
no one knew she was. And they certainly did not know
the circumstances, that *she had been unfaithful.* I looked
to see if anyone heard me think that.

I was so self-conscious.

Mary was not in the balcony.

I looked.

More than once.

"Rabbi Mattaniah, I need to talk to you privately," I said as
I left that day. Father cringed.

"Yes, of course, Joseph. I know all about it." I was stunned.
Stopped in my tracks. How could he know? When did
he find out? Who else knew?

"You know?"

"Yes, my son. I was young once too. Joseph, are you all
right?" The color had poured from my face.

"Fine, Rabbi, I'm, well, I'll be fine. I just need to see you."

"Tomorrow, then. Come round first thing, we will talk." He
was smiling. I was not.

Another day could easily kill me.

Another sleepless night would be the end of my sanity.

It stormed and thundered through the night.

It forced me to consider my choices.

I should avoid a public scandal.

Nothing would be gained.

That would avoid the humiliation.

I had the option to do this privately.

If I brought this out in the open, some would insist on a
public trial and, although there was little chance of a
public stoning, the thought made me ill.

Moses would have insisted,

but Moses is not here.

Still, I have feelings for Mary. More than just feelings.

I had to admit I still love her,

but I could not bear the thought of trying to pretend
this—that I could somehow deal with this.

The Decision

What kind of a monster would I be? To have Mary stoned
was to murder this unborn child.

That would be a double murder.

So, my mind was made up.

A private letter of divorce. Could I ...?

Yes, perfect, I will make a provision of the divorce, that Mary
should head right back to spend the remaining time with
Elizabeth and the whole scandal could be avoided.

Perhaps I could forget about this mess.

I was relieved at last.

A decision.

The decision that would be best for everyone.

It's not like this would matter at all in a few months.

I slept.

EIGHT
Secrets

"Joseph, son of David."

I tried to speak, to answer, but was paralyzed. I tried to force my eyes open. I struggled, but I couldn't move. Was I in danger? I woke with a start, sweating, soaked through. No one, nothing was there. Only the moonlight from the window and a wisp of air flowing through the curtains. Relief—just a dream—I dozed off.

"Joseph, son of David."

Again. Still I couldn't move. Was it Father trying to see if I was all right? If I had done anything foolish? I tried to wake, but my mind went blank.

"Joseph, son of David."

I only knew that this sounded familiar. I felt restless. I began to see something. Then it took form. A shape of sorts. I was sure I was seeing a man, but not like any man I had ever seen. More like a shadow—a bright shadow—by the window.

"Joseph, son of David, don't be afraid."

And, and I was not afraid.

"Don't be afraid to take Mary home as your wife."
    Time stopped.
    Don't be afraid to take Mary as my wife?
    Easy for him to say. He would not have to shrink under the stares and ignore the gossip.
"Joseph, what was conceived in her is from the Holy Spirit. She will give birth to a son, and you will give him the name Yeshua."
    Yeshua?
        There is no one in our family named Yeshua.
        I was planning on a Joseph junior.
"He will save his people from their sins."
    I waited for more. This was not Father. There was a sudden rush of wind and I was fully awake.
I ran those words through my mind,
    wondering if this was only a dream.
I could not have ever imagined anything like this.
    As desperate as I was for a solution, an answer, a way out,
        this was not it,
        even in my wildest dreams.
The angel said, "Don't be afraid to take Mary home as your wife."
    I wasn't afraid,
    I wasn't going to take her as my anything.

Suddenly, Samuel sprang to mind.

He was awakened in the night by someone calling his name.

Only the someone was the Lord.

Who do I talk to about this?

Would my rabbi believe me?

Rabbi!

I have an appointment with Rabbi Mattaniah.

But I had reached a decision.

A decision I was so sure of.

But the Lord,

or an angel of the Lord, appeared to me.

He called me "Son of David."

I knew I was in the legal line of the throne. And as the Son of David, I suppose I have responsibilities much larger than my own personal concerns.

"God, are you sure about this? There will be talk. How will we …?"

I was late for my appointment.

"Rabbi, here I am." He was on his walk.

"Come. Join me, Joseph. So what's on your mind, my friend, as if I don't know?"

"First, I want to thank you for seeing me and you have already encouraged me."

"Joseph, like I told you, I was young once. There was a girl, a beauty, that stole my heart."

"Rabbi, I'm shocked." I wasn't exactly shocked, but this language from my rabbi was out of character.

"I doubt that, son. Yes, my heart was torn between my studies and my romance."

"I confess, I never thought of you as a romantic."

"Do you think my marriage of fifty years is just for show?"

"No. I mean, I haven't thought about it."

"Well, you should think about others a little more often, Joseph. You are an important example in this community of ours, and you should behave as such."

This was not going to go well I was afraid. "That could complicate things, Rabbi. You see, Mary and I … "

"You think I haven't been put in this position before? Mary and you *must* get married right away. Is that what's on your heart?"

"Rabbi, what was the scripture reading yesterday?"

"Where were you? Oh, how youth is wasted on the young. Always such a hurry. Joseph, you will learn to be patient, or God will teach you the hard way. It was the prophet Isaiah, 'The virgin will be with child and will give birth to a son, and they will call him Immanuel.'"

I grabbed his shoulder and turned him to face me. "Sir, would this be speaking of the Messiah? The one who will take away our sin?"

"Who else, Joseph? Yes, I would say you understand."

"Rabbi, when will this be?"

"This is what you wanted to talk about, Joseph."

"No, well yes, not exactly."

"Thanks for clearing that up. Come, let's continue. No one knows the time nor the hour when such a thing will occur. But, mark my words, their lives will be in danger. This people of ours aren't ready to have their sins taken away," Rabbi blurted out.

"Sir?"

"Sorry, Joseph. I shouldn't have been so abrupt. This is not for your ears. Our secret, please."

"Certainly, sir, and I have one for you. I'm not sure how to put it."

"Just *put it,* Joseph, I trust you. You are in the lineage of our King David as I remember, and I suspect God has a special purpose for you. One more thing, it is better that a man marry than burn in his desire and sin against God."

It was like I was not here,
        but hearing this.

First the scripture, a virgin giving birth to Messiah, then Rabbi reminding me of my lineage, responsibility, my duty to God, and then, did he just suggest to marry soon?

I wondered, *why, God, are you so merciful to me?*

"Joseph, did you hear me? What is it? What is your precious secret? If it is just that you want a speedy marriage, trust me, I understand. Most around here think I'm an old stick-in-the-muck, and I prefer it that way, but I've

58

been right in your sandals, my son. A year's betrothal is almost more than a man, or woman for that matter, can be expected to endure. With the Roman and pagan influences, the shameful manner of dress, and now brothels gaining a legitimacy, I suspect your, shall we say manhood, is driving you out of your mind. Am I right? You make a date. Make sure both families are in agreement."

My head was spinning. He did indeed say marry soon. This wasn't my question, but I felt this was a good time to keep quiet and take this good fortune and his grand advice.

"You look surprised, Joseph."

"Much more than that. I cannot begin to tell you how glad I am we had this talk, this time together."

"Mazel tov, Joseph. And, Joseph, then after the ceremony, perhaps you and Mary should get away for a while. In case there is talk. Perhaps that will help you both."

"Shalom, my friend, my Rabbi,
    you have given me great comfort."

"Shalom. Peace be with you. You give me hope."

Peace indeed. The first since ... I can't remember.
    I wondered if I could trust my ears.
    I had to wonder if he knew more than he revealed.
    And the scripture reading,
and he was so ready to answer my questions before I even asked.

I am a blessed man.

Wait till I see Mary—*Mary!* What must she think?
What am I thinking.
  What if she has changed her mind?
Joseph, stop it.
  There I go again.

I passed my house to see Mother and Father, only long enough
    to tell them it was going to be all right.
I didn't explain, but promised I would.
I stepped into my—*our* new house to change before seeing
    Mary.
I splashed water on my face.
When I looked up, there she was sitting in the garden.
  The garden I had destroyed.
She must have heard me come in, but was looking the other
    way when I walked out.
I sat across from her and took her hands in mine.
She was trembling.
I was sure I needed to say something quite brilliant, something
    quite perfect.
But that wasn't exactly my practice lately.
She looked at me straight on.
  She had been crying.
  I could see streaks on her beautiful face.
  Her eyes were swollen.
  Her cheeks flushed and blotched.
    I felt like dirt.

She was here in our home waiting for me.

She was soft and strong and magnificent.

My stomach churned.

She took my hand and placed it on her stomach.

It didn't seem odd at all.

"Yeshua," I said and her face lit up. "We will name him Yeshua."

"Mary, you must forgive me."

She pressed two fingers to my mouth and leaned closer.

She narrowed her eyes a bit.

They were glistening with tears that spilled down her cheeks, across her luscious lips.

She shook her head ever so slightly.

Then she slipped both her hands to my cheeks and kissed me full on the lips with her eyes wide open.

She did not speak.

That said it all.

"Joseph, shall we clean this up? It looks like a pack of wild animals have been through."

I placed two fingers on her mouth.

We laughed hard, and embraced harder.

"Mary, Rabbi Mattaniah urged me to—or I should say in-dicated—that he would approve going ahead with the wedding, the ceremony, most anytime."

"Won't everyone wonder? Won't they talk?"

"Mary, under the circumstances, a little talk now might … "

"Yes, I know you are right, and I can still wear my regular clothes for another six weeks or so. You may leave it to me. No one will suspect. I will be able to hide this easy."

"Then it's settled. We're betrothed for nearly five months … "

"Joseph, it's barely four." Mary grinned.

"Like I said, we are in our fifth month."

"Have it your way." Mary was pleased. "So, when are you thinking?"

"Next month, the very first of the month. That will be the sixth month."

"You will only give me four weeks to plan a wedding. What will everyone think?"

"We discussed that I think. And we only need to concern ourselves with what God thinks."

"My spiritual husband."

"My beautiful bride. Mary, the scripture reading, I forgot to tell you … "

"Father told me. He was there."

"Isaiah: 'The virgin will be with child and will give birth to a son, and they will call him Immanuel.'"

"Yes, I know Joseph. Is that what convinced you?"

"That, and the fact that I could not live without you."

"Joseph, you wouldn't be stretching the truth now, would you?"

"Well, there was this little visit from an angel of the Lord."

"Angel? You didn't tell me about an angel."

I hadn't.

I didn't think for a minute about telling anyone. It seemed so personal. *Who would believe me?*

"Joseph, I didn't tell you about my angel either."

We had much to confess.

"Mary, how can we do this? We are so normal, so plain, so unprepared."

"With God, nothing is impossible, my husband. And you, Joseph, have the most difficult task of all. Most men would run the other way and never look back. Now you must wait. We must wait to consummate our marriage. I know that will be difficult for you, and for me also, my husband."

"Mary no. I know—we will just pray that God will give us joy in waiting. Mary, there's more, Isaiah said, 'For unto us a child is born, unto us a son is given, and the government shall be upon his shoulder; and his name shall be called Wonderful, Counselor, The Mighty God, The Everlasting Father, The Prince of Peace.' Mary—that's our Yeshua. How can we raise a Messiah?"

"And how, why now, would God choose us, my husband?"

The wedding was on.

The house of Heli was in a frenzy.

Mother spent all her time with Lois and Mary. I have never seen her so beside herself.

"Joseph, this will be a special child."

"You have no idea, Mother."

That was the last Mary and me spoke till our wedding day, that I can remember.

That was the last I heard from any of the women.

Suddenly I was not necessary to any of them.

Mary would smile with a glint in her eye—if I saw her at all. She rather enjoyed teasing me.

I spent my time putting finishing touches on the house and building, finishing, the most priceless crib the world has ever seen.

For the most precious child the world would ever know.

Even as that thought filled my mind, I couldn't grasp what I was thinking.

Many ask, "Why so soon?"

I told them all, "I'm not getting any younger."

Only Phinehas asked the most delicate question.

"Joseph, what is the real reason for the rush? You can tell me. It is not a sin to … when you are betrothed, it is permissible." He was baiting me.

Regulations may be changing, but not for me and my Mary.

"Would you stand up for me at our wedding, Phinehas?"

"Me?" You should have seen the look on his face. "You mean it? Yes. Yes, I will. I would be honored. Of all people, you pick me?"

"And I would be honored to have you. As far as your other question … "

"Oh, never mind that. I was just being—never mind. Like you say, you're not getting any younger."

Amazing, how smart I am when I know God's will.

Secrets

I prayed so often,
 seeking, wanting God's purpose for my life.
Too many times I prayed, thinking my ritual prayer would
 please God.
Too many times I wonder if anyone can know God's will.
 Moses, Isaiah, Jeremiah, the prophets,
  but I'm no prophet.
Oh my! I may not be a prophet,
 but soon to see prophecy with my own eyes.
 I am an instrument of Holy God.
 Jehovah Eleohim.
 Almighty God.
How can this be?
 Why would God entrust me?
 I must stop questioning and trust. As I told Mary,
 since this is God,
  I must not, need not, ask so many questions.
Why comes to mind constantly.
 Answers came with more questions.
My peace came as a surprise. A welcomed surprise.
 A quiet knowing.
Even Father was proud of my new confidence.
 It wasn't a conscious effort.
I spent the first hour, many mornings, meeting with Rabbi
 Mattaniah, searching and discussing the Messiah's com-
 ing, the hope of Israel.
He welcomed me, was eager to see me.
 Suspicious at first.

I so wanted to tell him the whole truth. But had no peace about that.

We became great friends.

He's a great scholar.

His appearance of a stuffy, crusty old relic was one of convenience, he confessed.

"If a man is serious about his God, I will know." He said.

"Too many are just lazy. They want me to have all the answers. They are babies. They forgot to grow up. They expect to be fed, but there comes a time to feed yourself. I want folks to know their God, not just my God."

"There's a difference?"

"Don't disappoint me, Joseph. But I sympathize. Rabbis, most rabbis, want you to only know *their* God. That's what nearly got me kicked out of rabbinical school. I asked too many questions. I argued too often. I was too excited about a living God. One that only I wanted to resurrect."

"What happened? What did you do, Rabbi?"

"I learned to ask questions of myself. I waited. I finished my studies, and this is where I was relegated. How much farther from Jerusalem could they send me? Little did they realize, it sent me further in my search for answers to my many questions."

"Jerusalem? You were trained in Jerusalem?"

"Trained, dismissed, and forgotten, I imagine. I fear I went from a has-been to a never-was."

I had to chuckle. "Did you find your answers?"

Rabbi cocked his head. He looked frustrated that I asked this. Then, stared off.

"Some, I suppose, Joseph. But you are my redemption."

"Excuse me?"

He had my attention.

"Joseph, how many I have seen over the years just going through the motions. They think they please, satisfy God, with their appearance, their attendance or tithe. Little do they know, I'm afraid to say, the heart of God. But you have given me hope. You ask bright questions, and in earnest. You ask some dull ones too, but I know you ask them with a pure heart. Mary is a blessed woman. You will make a fine husband, and a fine father."

"From your mouth to God's ears, kind sir."

"Amein. And Joseph, our secret."

"Amein, Amein. Shalom."

I didn't say, *I will make a fine father sooner than you think.*

I was tempted.

NINE
Three Pieces

It was raining when I woke on my wedding day.
    Not a good sign.
But then the rainbow. A very good sign.
"Thank you, Noah. And you too, Jehovah."

Just a few hours now.
    Father knocked, and entered.
We did not know what to say. Awkward for a time.
He wanted to be something he needed to be, for me.
Finally I told him, "Relax already," and we both laughed.
He was the one anxious and I like a calm sea.

Both of our families regretted not having the expected five
    day celebration, but not Mary.
It was as if she wasn't interested in the ceremony at all,
    not like most brides.
Of course Mary's family were just humble folks, and I cer-
    tainly didn't have much left in the way of savings, just
    finishing the house, and now with the baby coming, I

had to confess, "Mary, I don't know how in the world we're going to make ends meet. I didn't plan on a baby so soon."

"Did I? For goodness sake, it will be fine, it will be just fine."

The chatan, the groom—that's me—fast on this day until sundown, until the wedding feast.

As does the kallah, the bride, that's Mary. She would need to eat for the child, but would not for herself. I'm not sure how she did that.

For us, we were celebrating a personal Yom Kippur, day of atonement from our sins. Kabbalat Panim was tradition for the bride and groom, to refrain from seeing each other for the entire week preceding the wedding. We tried, we wanted to, we failed, and asked for forgiveness.

The ceremony was small, but more than adequate.

Rabbi Mattaniah was more than perfect.

He surprised us with his humor, a side of him that we never heard in temple.

It was just family and a few close friends.

Even so, the guest list seemed to have a life all its own.

Mother and Father and I met Mary and her mother and father to begin the ceremony.

Phinehas waited impatiently at the chupah, the marriage canopy.

Mary didn't look pregnant at all.

The flowing lace and the flowers in her hand hid any hint.
The traditions, the important ones, were kept.
We began the procession through the gathering in the garden
    of our new home.
That was not tradition, but the temple grounds were in the
    center of town and a full legion of Romans had arrived
    and set up camp nearby. No one knew why.

Stars beamed and the moon reflected a perfect glow on this
    beautiful setting.
Having the wedding here at our home would make a good
    excuse for our guests to leave without undue delay.
I lifted her veil to see my bride.
I waited—and replaced the veil.
    It was Mary.
This tradition, "the badeken," is in remembrance of poor
    Jacob who was tricked into marrying Leah. She was hid-
    ing under the veil, instead of his love, Leah's younger
    sister, Rachel.
The veiling also provides that no matter how beautiful Mary
    may be, the beauty of her soul is most important.
But Mary's veil could never hide her radiance, her charm.
Her hair was all ringlets filled with the tiniest white flower
    buds. Her gown of white linen was layered with lace
    and ribbons.
Rabbi winked at me, more than once.
He'd sampled the wine, more than once.

Three Pieces

The chupah was just perfect. Its four poles were draped and
    entwined with vines in bloom.
We would enter this canopy for the formalities to symbolize
    creating our new home together, just as did Abraham
    and Sarah.
Rabbi Mattaniah was beaming.
I remembered how I fretted that he would be indignant at
    my request for a hurried ceremony, yet here he is in his
    finest.
He placed the rolled and bound ketubah, our contract that
    he personally prepared, in outstretched hands.
Just as our heavenly Father created our world in seven days,
    Mary began to circle me for seven times to show we are
    creating a new world for us. Rabbi recited the seven
    blessings, the kiddushin.
We drank from the cup, and I recited my vows.
"I will betroth thee unto me forever; yea, I will betroth thee
    unto me in righteousness, and in justice, and in loving
    kindness, and in mercies. I will even betroth thee unto
    me in faithfulness; and thou shall know Jehovah. And
    it shall come to pass in that day, I will answer, so says
    Jehovah, according to the prophet Hosea."

Now, I had a surprise for Mary.
She never expected, she told me so.
I handed the ketubah to Rabbi.
I lifted Mary's veil again, for the last time.

I turned to Phinehas for the ring, he was ready.

"Joseph!" Mary gasped.

The ring cost a small fortune, but this marriage priceless.

The ring was pure gold, to show I have the purest love.

The ring was without seam, without beginning or end, just as our marriage could not be broken, and is without end.

"Mary, behold, you are betrothed unto me with this ring, according to the Law of Moses and Israel."

She was trembling when I placed the ring on her finger. I kissed her for the first time as her husband, her protector, her comforter, her lover.

Rabbi read the ketubah, and we drank again from the cup.

He took the matzo, the unleavened bread, and tore it into three pieces.

"You break your fast with sanctified bread as you begin your holy union."

He placed a piece in my hand.

He repeated to Mary,

"You break your fast with sanctified bread as you begin your holy union."

Then he took the third piece. "Save this for Messiah, the holy one sure to come as our salvation." He placed it in Mary's hand. I wondered if he knew how true this was?

He uncovered the wine glass and held it for all to see.

"The wedding is complete. The two have become one. We are to be one with our God and must never forget the destruction of our holy temple."

He placed the cup between us.

Three Pieces

He placed the cloth over the cup.
I took Mary's hand and we faced our guests.
"Mary," I said to her alone, "Our love will endure. This cup
    I break to say to you, all our enemies will be smashed
    and scattered to pieces."
I stomped the glass.

    "Mazel tov!"

Our guests were ready,
    They cheered, and the singing and music erupted.
The dishes of cakes and dates and delicacies were uncovered
    as the children dashed for their favorites.
The festivities began.

    But not for long.

TEN
What Does This Mean?

Jonah snarled.

We felt a trembling underfoot.

    We heard horses in a hurry.

    The whole party flooded through the house and out front.

    We stopped as a dozen soldiers halted, and they spread out side by side.

    Massive men on sweating, foul smelling animals.

    Mary was trembling again. I was angry.

    The horses were snorting and straining at their reins.

    The Romans were laughing and sneering and pointing.

    I was ready to protect, but I didn't like my odds.

    I pulled Mary behind me. If they wanted her, it would be over my dead body.

    My pulse was pounding. Ringing in my ears.

The centurion unfurled a scroll and read:

"Take heed, take heed.
Hear this day all who abide in the world of Caesar Augustus,
the most gracious and righteous Emperor of Rome.

74

What Does This Mean?

**EACH ONE WILL BE INSCRIBED TO THE CENSUS OF HIS MAJESTY
BY PROVINCE OF HEROD, YOUR KING OF JUDEA.
MAKE WAY TO THE HOUSE OF YOUR LINEAGE.
ALL PERSONS IN THE SOUND OF MY VOICE, JEW OR GENTILE,
SLAVE OR FREE, COMPLIANCE IS DECREED THIS DAY FORTH
IN THE LANDS AND POSSESSIONS OF HIS ROYAL AND GREAT CAESAR."**

"So sorry to break up your little party," another said. His voice
    dripped with sarcasm and the rest roared.
They jerked the horses about, but stood their ground to let
    us know who was in charge. One, in the center, unfurled
    his whip. Others placed a hand on their sword.
Their threat was all too obvious.
They were looking for trouble and hoping for an excuse to
    shed some blood. Some Jewish blood.

"May I say a blessing on you fine fellows?" Rabbi Mattaniah
    spoke up to my amazement. He caught the thugs off guard.
They looked disappointed that no one challenged them.
Still, we were outnumbered, unarmed,
    and ill-equipped for the likes of these.
We retreated to the house and gardens. Our guests began to
    leave as the detachment pranced away, shouting insults
    over their shoulders.

"Joseph, what does this mean?"
"We should pack and leave. The sooner we leave, the sooner
    we can return."

"Leave? To where?"
"Bethlehem, Mary. Bethlehem."

All the way to Bethlehem was a sobering thought.
Travel these days, well, it's best to have a caravan or at least an escort. Tale after tale of travelers robbed and beaten and left to die in ditches.
And now with the Roman presence, bullies pushing folks around. Life was not the same. Nazareth had become a military outpost, and now we knew why.

"Joseph, dear Joseph, our beautiful home ... "
"It will be here when we return. With any good fortune, we will be back inside of a month. Rabbi even suggested we should go away for a time. Perhaps God has provided a way for us to do just that."
"But, my husband, we have a child to think of. Are we, will we be in danger? Will he?"
"God would not give us anything that we can't handle." I tried to sound more confident than I felt.
"Then it will be just fine." Mary said with some assurance.
    I felt the burden.

I wanted to ask, "Why God? Why now? Why, if we are called by you, do things become so—complicated?"
I wanted to ask, but I didn't think God owed me an answer.

ELEVEN
Five Days - Five Months

We packed a few things. Heli brought fresh baked flat bread. Neighbors brought bags of lentils. Goatskins filled with water and a splash of wine. Dried meats, dates, figs, and salted fish were strung on leather cords. I packed some tools just in case.

Father said to take the donkey. "You will have to stand in for us in Bethlehem, Mother cannot possibly make the journey." This was obvious after a fall last spring, she had difficulty walking, even with her staff.

"Of course, Father. I will say our goodbyes now. We leave at first light. But this is barely a colt. Has she been ridden?"

"She's very mild mannered, I'm sure she will be easily trained. You are not going alone, just the two of you?"

"No. There will be many headed our way. We will join them, Father. I best leave Jonah with you."

We traveled east, south of Nain and just north of Mount Gilboa through Scythopolis, another military outpost that showed signs of turning into a Roman province with prostitutes working the roads in broad daylight.

Times are changing.

Mary looked the other way. We purposely avoided Arippina for this very reason. Now we had to overnight in a hostel.

The company we joined was a comfort to us both, but the children ran wild and were a nuisance in a short time.

The next day, half of their troop had disappeared with some of our food stock as well.

"Just when you think you can trust someone. How is it, Mary, when we are called by God, on his mission, for his purpose, do you realize how many things have gone wrong?"

"Joseph, somehow I know, it will be just fine."

If she says that one more time, I'll ...,

"Mary, if you would feel better, we can head right back to Nazareth and restock. Perhaps we left a bit hastily."

"Joseph, it's your decision, but I think we will be ..."

"I know Mary. I agree. We will be fine."

We ate a bit of breadcakes, brewed some tea, and left straight out for the Jordan to join the trade routes south. I could net us some fish, and perhaps find some work.

At least the donkey was here and my tools in place.

At the banks of the Jordan we found a settlement.

Mary recognized a young family she had traveled with on her way home from seeing Elizabeth.

Elated to see her and to meet me, they quickly unloaded our donkey, ushered us to the roof, and insisted we stay with them for awhile, before we had time to object.

"Joseph, you are a carpenter I understand." Caleb, the man of the house, obviously knew something of me.

"Yes, Caleb, do you need something tended to?"

"Yes, you could say that. I am not the handiest man in town."

Selah, his wife giggled. "But, you are the most handsome, my husband."

They were a joy to be around.

"Mary, how pregnant are you?" Women know these things.

"Not much," Mary said and looked at me with raised eyes.

"I'd say you are completely pregnant." Selah had a point.

One day turned into a week and then some.

Caleb seemed to thrive on finding work for me. He was a good businessman.

The next thing I know we felt like family and none suspected anything amiss about our pending birth. Mary was at peace. Soon we had recovered our losses and about to move on when I received word that Mother was gravely ill.

"Joseph, you go," Mary insisted. "I can stay here. I do not want to face the town or have to explain, with my morning sickness and all ... you know."

"What will I say?"

"You will think of something, husband, you always do." Mary was smiling, and I was relieved.

It would be simpler for me to go alone and tend to things, check on the house, and such.

Mother withered. One month, then two.
    She was brave, but her paralysis was relentless.
        The physicians offered little hope.
Father was determined to spend every waking moment at her side, so I had my hands full with visitors, chores, and unfinished business.
The constant questions of "Where's Mary?" were fading.
I traveled back or sent word to her every few days.
Lots of travelers these days, and most ready to pick up some loose coins for the simple job as courier.

One morning I arrived to find Father in the front yard waiting for me.
"Joseph, your mother ... her suffering is over."
"And yours as well, Father."
"Yes, mine as well."
After the period of mourning, it was time to leave.
"I'll be back as soon as the Lord allows, Father."
"You be careful, son. Can't wait till you return. Don't forget I love you. You're all I have left."
Father was becoming sentimental.
    I was glad he had Jonah.

I'm not sure what he's going to do without Mom. If I didn't have Mary, I'm not so sure what I would do. And if something happens to Mary—perhaps I should treat her as if something could happen to her. Mom's death challenged me to think about what is really important in life.

That eased my mourning.

All the way back to Jordan memories of Mom persisted. I don't remember an argument between her and Father. She would often be frustrated with me, but not angry. She took up for me if Father was being a bit stern, but she left the room if I was about to get a thrashing for something we all knew I deserved.

Most of all she had the greatest smile. It was full of joy, delight and approval. Her smile was always the first thing to greet me. She loved it when I came in the room. We lost my older brother when he was but nine years old and Father said she doted on me entirely too much, but he picked up that habit in the last few years too. I couldn't help but think, right out of Torah, the very first book, God said, "and the two shall become one."

I am that one.

I am my father and mother's boy.

I almost talked Mary into staying while I headed to Bethlehem without her.

"Joseph, I'll be just fine."

"I thought you might say that." *I think she missed me.*
　　Off we went.

We did not expect it would be sheer torture for Mary.
　　This baby, this pregnancy, was taking its toll.
We expected four days travel,
　　five at the most.
It would be three full days just to make Cypress.
Normally we would have gone through Jericho, but I thought
　　the climb would be too much for Mary and the donkey.
　　I extended our trip south of Bethany to avoid the hills,
　　and then on into Bethlehem.
It was a good decision except longer than I hoped.
It was already late as we approached Bethany.
We had joined a family, with three sons so large they looked
　　like they could take on a small army. They knew the best
　　route and offered to give us an overnight stay, but Mary
　　objected. "Joseph, no, please let's continue. I don't think
　　I can stand another day's travel."
We moved on.
Mary was half asleep, jostling on the donkey.
I wondered if we would ever reach Bethlehem. Not just the
　　town of my lineage, my birthplace as well. I was glad to
　　be going there, but not under these circumstances. I knew
　　this census was just a ploy by Rome to disinherit rightful
　　heirs of their property and holdings.

I wrapped a blanket around Mary.

She was shivering and in pain.

I calculated the time. Astonished to realize the birth could be anytime within the next two weeks.

I stopped ... with a horrifying thought.

It made me shudder.

"What is it, Joseph?"

"Nothing. Nothing at all." I lied.

But, it was something. I just realized, as much as God wants his Messiah to be born to save his people, there is evil and this is the last thing the enemy of our souls, the devil, wants.

I never felt more intimidated by the darkness surrounding us.

It fell on me like a covering of mold, musty, alive, heavy on my shoulders. Fatigue engulfed me.

Dizzy.

Anguish filled my thoughts.

I have made a terrible mistake and now I'm paying for it.

I was tempted to stop and give up. Useless.

No!, I told myself. I felt an urgency to reach our destination.

One foot forward.

Another.

I pressed on.

There were lights in the distance.

Just over the horizon. Lights, it must be.

It just must be.

TWELVE
The Stable

When we reached the City of David, Bethlehem, I had trouble
believing we were in the right city. Noise and shouting
and music in the middle of the night.
Morning really.

"Joseph, hurry please—Joseph? What is going on in this
town?"
"Mary, I can't believe it myself, but apparently Bethlehem is
much more than just sheep and shepherds these days."

It had been years since I was here, and I had no idea.
There was a tent city with sounds of a festival.
People milled around aimlessly.

"Joseph, please."
I stopped at the first house that had a sign: "Rooms."
"You must be joking" the man laughed slamming the door
only to reopen it.
I had a glimmer of hope.

The Stable

But he snatched the sign inside, and slammed the door harder.
The next stop was a sizable hostel, but there was no light and
    I wasn't sure if I should disturb anyone.
        I didn't have much choice.
I knocked. An obscene shout came from the second floor,
    I won't repeat it.
Inn after inn. House after house.
    Nothing.

"Joseph?"
"Any minute now, Mary. Any minute." I lied.
    What hope I had, faded three stops ago.
    Everywhere I looked there were horses and donkeys and
    carts, but no rooms.
At one place, the innkeeper said, "Take our room." But he
    wanted so much money, we would be broke in two days.

Then, near the far end of town I spotted one last inn.
    One last hope.
    I knocked. I knocked again. I waited.
"If you ain't got a reservation, you ain't got a room," a scruffy
    little man barked behind the half open door.
    I stood there.
"Did you hear me?" I heard him. I turned to leave.
        I'd run out of ideas. I'd run out of town.
        I hadn't thought to pack a tent.
Mary groaned. She gasped.

She yelled and slumped hard against the donkey's neck, clutching her stomach, grasping the bridle to keep from falling.

She clinched her eyes, choking back another scream.

I rushed to her side.

"Wait. Just wait." I turned to see the innkeeper reach for a lantern and start round the side. "Follow me."

And we did. I should say we followed his odor.

He reeked of ale and such.

I steadied Mary best I could.

He staggered, stopped in front of a stable out back.

"A stable? A stinking stable? Is this a joke?"

I wanted to strangle this man.

My patience, my nerves, my faith were spent.

My bride in pain.

My head pounding.

"Any place, Joseph. Any place will be just fine." Mary was sliding off her mount. It was all I could do to catch her.

Her arm felt on fire. Her face was flushed.

I was so angry, useless and tired.

How could I let this happen?

"Fresh hay there. Stream that-a-way. G'night." The smelly little man held out the lantern. I took it. He left.

Mary sank on a fresh pile of hay just inside while I held the light to see the rest of this little grotto.

It could have been worse.

The Stable

The three stalls were clean.
  A cow stared.
I unloaded our bags, sacks and blankets, and prepared a place
  for Mary to lie down. I helped her the best I could. She
  held my neck as I lowered her onto the bedroll. I don't
  remember being more exhausted.
"Mary, I am so sorry." She pressed two fingers to my lips,
  kissed them, and then collapsed.

I fed our donkey. I looked to the heavens.
"Are you there? Have you forgotten us, forgotten Mary? Do
  you see the mess we are in?"
I had to shake my head in bewilderment.
I squatted and leaned my head against my staff,
    feeling like a fool,
        a failure.

A scream startled me from my stupor.
    Then a cry.
        A baby's cry.

I shook the fog from my head and nearly fell on my face.
Mary—she was half sitting, half reclining against a pile of hay
  holding a child. A beautiful child.
"Mary?"
"Joseph, look."
    How could I not look?

There she was sitting, swaying, with a beautiful baby in her
arms.

"Yeshua, our Yeshua has arrived," I said. I felt like a king.

"It was a miracle. I was nearly asleep when here he comes. I
was amazed." Mary beamed.

"But you hardly screamed."

"There was pain. Not so much. Well, plenty to be sure, but,
Joseph I kept thinking, 'Unto us a child is born ... '"

"'Unto us a son is given.'" The verse sprang to life in my heart.

"'And the government will be on his shoulder,'" Mary added.

"'And his name shall be called Wonderful, Counselor, The
Mighty God, The Everlasting Father, The Prince of
Peace,'" we said together—almost shouting.

"Mary, isn't God amazing?"

"Look at all he provided." She held the little bundle up for
me to take. I had to grin.

"Yeshua," I said. "Look at all he provided.
We came on a borrowed donkey.
We are in a borrowed stable.
And I suppose I better find you a crib.
It will be borrowed too."

My fear and anger were gone. I knew many had less than we.
I apologized to God and thanked him, thinking, *what if we
didn't have the stable?*

There was a manger. A little thing.

The Stable

It looked new. It would do just fine. I smiled when I
thought that. Exactly what Mary would say—*just fine*.
But, not nearly as fine as the one I left behind.
I cleaned the manger, covered the hay, and set it beside Mary.
I helped her clean up. I brought her a clean blanket. I built
a small fire, snuffed out the lantern, lay down beside my
bride, and wrapped my arms around her in wonder of her
strength and faith and beauty.

The birth of a child, this child. So amazing. Such a miracle.
I wanted to ask God.
Why, why, why?
Why should the savior be born in a stable?
Why not a palace?
Why should the savior have common, ordinary parents?
Why not a king and queen?
Why should the savior be born in obscurity?
Why not in a cloud of angels?
Why now?
Here?
To us?
I wanted to ask God these things,
but somehow it all seemed unimportant just now.

Just as night gave way to dawn we had company.
Shepherds. Seven in all.

"Are you ... ? Is this ... ?" The shepherd's excitement was shared by his company. "Sorry sir, we can explain. We're looking for a baby in a manger."

Mary and I were amused. I couldn't help but wonder, did they know—and how?

"Yes, please come in. You are welcome. And, why are you here?"

"We were in the fields," he said, "when the heavens opened, an angel appeared ... "

"We were frightened for our lives," another added.

Mary and I looked at each other and smiled.

She was so radiant.

I knew God had sent us another confirmation.

"An angel, you say?" I taunted him a bit.

"I know, it sounds ridiculous," a third joined in, "But it's true."

"We all saw it," still another said and pushed forward.

"An angel." The elder of the group raised his arms, "And then a host of angels."

I thought maybe I should tell them, we know something of angels.

"Maybe we are in the wrong place." A woman's voice from the back offered.

"No, no. Here. See. A manger," I said. "Would you like to see the baby?"

They flooded by me to see Yeshua. It made me proud, even if I was completely unnecessary at the moment.

"Thank you, Lord," I said aloud, but only the Lord heard, I was sure.

The Stable

"Your child. This child is Messiah, the Lord. Our Savior." I couldn't tell, was he trying to convince me or himself? He was frustrated that I wasn't as excited as he.

"Yes, I know. But what makes you so sure?" I wanted to hear this.

"The angel told us straight out, *'This will be a sign to you: You will find the babe wrapped in swaddling clothes, and lying in a manger.'*" His voice filled with awe, his leathered face softened.

"I apologize, what are you called?"

"My name is Aaron, and no apology is necessary. And this is my family. My brothers; this is Jeheil, and there is Gahazi, and here is Benaial, and Elliab and our father and mother, our youngest, Bozra, is in the fields. And you are?" The shepherds were gracious, their eyes bright and full of life.

"I am Joseph, and this is my Mary and our son, Yeshua."

"Yeshua." Such a common name for a Savior. "Why Yeshua?"

A good question, I hadn't even asked that myself.

"An angel's instruction." I answered, as if it was the most normal of things to say.

"Then Yeshua it is," Aaron said with respect.

They gathered themselves up and left saying, "Glory to God in the highest."

God knew,
    we needed this visit as much as the shepherds did.

THIRTEEN
The Innkeeper

The town awoke.

The sun sprayed its welcomed heat on my face.

Mary was nursing Yeshua, and I was struck with the glorious
sight and a stunning thought, my wife nursing my savior.

Folks began to stir, stretching and yawning, washing their
faces and tramping off to the latrine.

I stoked the fire and warmed some goat milk and breadcakes.
I fetched some grain from our packs and made a mush
for Mary and me.

She handed me Yeshua so she could get up and tend to herself.

I was so proud of her. Amazed really.

And here I am holding Yeshua. Talk about amazing.

A baby. A son. The son of God. A savior. My savior too.

Too much for my mind to grasp.

"Morning, Joseph."

The smelly little innkeeper was back.

I handed Yeshua to Mary and poked the embers of our little
fire remembering how I wanted to strangle this little man.

The Innkeeper

But, he gave us shelter when we needed it the most.

"Morning." I answered.

"Hadad, my name is Hadad, the owner here."

He looked a fright. Obviously a long night for him, but he
    held some wonderful smelling bread wrapped in a cloth.

I was starving for real food.

"Hadad, come meet my wife, Mary and our newborn."

"Newborn?"

"Yes, see, just after you left, it began."

Hadad's face went blank.

"Is that for us, Mr. Hadad?" Mary broke the silence.

"Huh? Oh yes. Bread, butter, and tea. You might put the teapot
    on your fire. It may be cold. And honey. Real good honey."

"Thank you for the wonderful treat," Mary said.

I placed the food on a bench and the pot on the embers. "I
    hope you don't mind. I cleaned out your little manger
    and borrowed it for a crib. I made sure your animals had
    hay," I told him.

Hadad didn't respond. He stared at Yeshua.

"You want to hold him, Mr. Hadad?" Mary said.

"Yes." Hadad bent over as Mary handed Yeshua to him.

I wondered why he was so anxious to hold our child.

It looked to me that he didn't have any idea what he was
    doing, or how to do it. He cradled our baby like he was
    holding firewood.

But it was obvious he was enjoying himself.

"Yeshua. His name is Yeshua."

"Yeshua. Good morning, Yeshua. Sleep well?" The innkeeper swooned, entranced with Yeshua.

"Hadad! Where are you?" A woman's shrill voice came from the inn.

"I have to go now. Please stay as long as you like. Let me know if there is anything you need." Hadad started toward the inn. Holding Yeshua.

"Hadad?" I scolded for fun. He turned back.

"Yes?" He seemed to be torn between going to the inn and staying right where he was.

"Should you leave Yeshua with us?"

"Oh. Yes, of course. Sorry. Here. See you soon. Let me know if there … you know."

"Hadad." She called again. Hadad scampered off.

Mary and I laughed as we slathered a very large piece of bread with butter.

I poured hot tea and thanked God for this place and this food and even for our new friend, Hadad.

I put our faithful donkey in the fields nearby, then began making this hole in the hill tolerable. I had just begun rummaging through the sacks to gather our clothing and blankets and do some washing when Hadad was back.

"Joseph, Joseph, I have news." He was definitely back. "I just talked to my friend Jared. He has a cottage, small, no tiny, well very little it is, but vacant and the rent is nothing, nearly nothing and the deposit, there is no deposit, and you and Mary and Yeshua should go there." Hadad was very convincing.

"Hadad, I don't know what to say. We are just here for the census and then headed back."

"Now, you can't be going anywhere for awhile with the little baby and your wife just having it and all."

He had a good point.

Hadad began dragging out our bags and sacks and things before I could argue.

"Hadad, I don't think Mary will be able to move today."

"Well, how about a wagon? Jared has a wagon. I'll hitch it up. No one should stay here in this stinking stable, not with a brand new baby."

Another good point.

Mary raised her eyes in surprise at his sudden change of heart.

"Come, it's all set. I will fetch your things. You should keep that little manger. It's really too little for anything. I will get another made up."

"Perhaps I could do that for you."

"You? You a carpenter?"

"That's right Hadad, just a carpenter."

"Just? Joseph, we have only one carpenter in the whole of Bethlehem and he's always backed up—not an easy man. He's owed me a manger for months. He loaned me that pitiful one you're using for a crib. Just a carpenter?

"Joseph, you will be the most popular tradesman in Bethlehem."

Mary looked a little smug.
smiling at me,
    rocking Yeshua.
I read her lips as she whispered, "Thank you, God, that will
    be just fine."

We went from bride and bridegroom to mother and father.
    From homeless to tenant.
    From despair to joy.
    From doubts to promises.
    From jobless to most popular,
        well, I would have to see about that.

FOURTEEN
The Covenant

Hadad was tireless. He moved our belongings, modest as they were. He brought the crib and the donkey and listen to this, he even had hay delivered.

The cottage was two small rooms, but had a canvas covered shelter in the back courtyard.

The shed was overgrown with weeds, but would serve well for storing wood and tools if indeed I should find a job or two.

We met Jared. After Hadad cornered him, Jared said the first month's rent could wait.

More good news.

Jared helped me clear out the old shed and we discovered a rusty saw under the remnants of a splintered chest.

"Do you know the best man to purchase some wood stock, Jared? And, do we have a temple in town?"

Jared jerked his head and looked perplexed.

"Temple?"

"Yes, temple, and someone I can purchase some lumber from."

Jared thought. "I'm sure Ira would know about the wood. And there is a temple, but sorry, I don't know much about temples. Are you folks, religious, or something."

"I don't know about that, but we enjoy keeping the Sabbath. And we want to meet your rabbi for Yeshua's circumcision, and who is Ira?"

"Circumcision, of course, I didn't think of that. Yes, of course. And Ira is our carpenter. You'll pass his shop on the way to temple, the other side of those tents."

Jared seemed relieved.

I went to temple on Shabbat. Mary could not of course, because of her uncleanness. The law of Moses was very clear as recorded in the Scriptures of Leviticus:

"The Lord said to Moses, Say to the people of Israel,
If a woman conceives, and bears a male child,
then she shall be unclean seven days;
as at the time of her menstruation, she shall be unclean,
And on the eighth day the flesh
of his foreskin shall be circumcised.
Then she shall continue for thirty-three days in the blood
of her purifying; she shall not touch any hallowed
thing, nor come into the sanctuary,
until the days of her purifying are completed."

I spoke with Rabbi Hadoram and made the arrangements.

The Covenant

I wondered ... should I trust him with who our child is?

I chose to wait.

"But, Joseph, we should have the ceremony here. We could
have a reception." Mary was quite certain about this. "I
can't possibly think of not ... "

"Mary, the Savior circumcised outside of the temple?"

"He was born in a stable."

She had a good point.

"That we had no control over. This we do. Tradition.

Why start people talking?

Mary—I have an idea. We will go to Jerusalem upon your
purification and dedicate Yeshua to the Lord there. You
will be able to travel by then I'm sure. That will fulfill the
law."

And I hoped would satisfy my bride.

She breathed a sigh. "Yes, my husband. Yes. Thank you."

I began to see,

raising a child could cause friction in this family.

Hadad came with us to the circumcision.

He was beaming,

but then so was I.

Mary waited just outside in Jared's cart,

but could hear everything.

When Rabbi Hadoram saw Hadad, "You managed to have
Hadad come to temple? That's a wonder."

Rabbi Hadoram washed his hands and then he washed mine. He placed his tallith over his head. Then he took mine and draped it over my head and my arms making a tent over Yeshua.

"Who brings this child to make this covenant?"

"His mother, and ... and his father." The rabbi looked curious when I stammered. But I had told the truth as we knew it. He looked through the open window with approval to Mary. She listened outside, careful not to spoil Shabbat and the temple for seven days.

"As God said to Abraham," Rabbi began with sincerity. "'Such shall be the covenant between Me and ...' what is the child's name, Joseph?"

"His name is Yeshua."

"As God said to Abraham," Rabbi began again.

"'Such shall be the covenant between
Me and you and Yeshua.
You are to follow, you shall keep,
every male among you shall be circumcised.
You shall circumcise the flesh of the foreskin,
and that shall be a sign of the covenant
between Me and you and Yeshua.'
According to the word of the Lord
as written and commanded
by Moses in the book of Genesis."

The Covenant

Rabbi Hadoram selected the doubled edge blade, the izmel,
    and with one stroke made the precise cut.
    We both waited for the cry.
        There was no cry.
Rabbi was expecting Yeshua to let loose a wail.
    I as well.
    All babies scream at the pain,
        the cut, the circumcision.
What is circumcision without the baby's cry?

Rabbi's knife and hand still poised in the air
    waiting for the cry.
    But none came.
"This was no ordinary Brit milah." Rabbi Hadoram said.
"This is no ordinary child, Rabbi."

FIFTEEN
The Dedication

Little Yeshua didn't cry that day.
>Yeshua didn't cry. Hardly ever,
>>since his birth.

We often felt we should apologize when neighbors asked,
"Your baby, your child, he doesn't cry?"

Mothers seemed jealous. They didn't like a newborn getting
all the attention, Mary explained. Especially a stranger's
newborn.

Neighbors lingered at his crib or begged to hold him.

Yeshua didn't mind. He enjoyed other babies, playful children
and even that smelly little Hadad.

We wanted to be normal parents, but wondered when Yeshua
would show who he really is.

Mary radiated with her joy in Yeshua.

She—we both—knew this child was sent from God, with a
purpose beyond our imagination. I was afraid she would
coddle and spoil him.

>But was that actually possible?

She wanted to protect him from any possible danger or sickness or discomfort.

But we wondered if that was the right thing to do.

"I'm just being a mother, Joseph." Mary reminded me every time I made a suggestion.

We were both hesitant to make decisions, but Yeshua didn't seem to mind.

He slept through the night almost immediately.

He had a ravenous appetite, which kept Mary hungry as well.

Hadad spent as much time at our house as he did at his. Jared was with him often.

"Hadad, why do you not have children of your own?" It was a delicate, perhaps impolite question, but he seemed so attached to Yeshua.

"Well, it isn't from not trying, I assure you." We chuckled at that. "Just nothing happened, and with the inn and the tavern and all, it's probably best."

"You are welcome here anytime, Hadad," Mary told him.

"That's good news, I tell you. I can't explain it. It has never happened before, but your boy is, I don't know how to put it, he has a spell over me."

"Well, I don't know about that, but you come by any time." And trust me, he did.

We didn't mind, but he felt the need to bring things and send things whether we needed them or not. Soon he became a part of our family.

Before I realized it, Hadad had sent several customers and a few prospects.

I welcomed the income.

Was glad to work with my hands on some of the finest wood I'd ever seen. The cedar from Hebron rivaled any from Lebanon. Bethlehem being just between Hebron and Jerusalem, you can imagine, only the finest wood would be taken to the Holy City.

Often I had first pick. I liked that.

Yeshua shared my love for wood. I should say the smell of wood. Whenever I was sawing or cutting and sanding or turning, he was underfoot. Fresh cut acacia or cedar has a wonderful fragrance and he giggled as chips flew over his little head.

When the time of Mary's purification was complete, she asked about the sacrifice for Yeshua's dedication.

"We will purchase doves or pigeons in Jerusalem," I explained, then Hadad arrived carrying a cage with two doves.

"Hadad, we have to purchase them ourselves, and the temple inspectors can be selective." He looked dejected.

"Joseph," Mary said. "There is no harm in taking these. If they're rejected, then they're rejected and we will purchase others there."

"A borrowed sacrifice? Mary, that is no sacrifice."

The Dedication

"Whatever you two decide." Hadad rushed to say. "But I bought these from the temple merchants. Or I should say my ale supplier bought them for me. I knew you would need them."

"An ale supplier? I don't know." It just didn't seem right. Not for Yeshua, I was sure.

"Ale suppliers need sanctification too." Hadad offered.

He sat the cage on the windowsill.

They cooed.

We were trapped.

Once again we borrowed the cart from Jared, hitched up our donkey and headed off to Jerusalem.

We would be in the Holy City midmorning and needed to find a priest for the ceremony. We agreed this fell at a good time.

Passover began with this coming Shabbat and we were ahead of the crowds. Most at least.

We followed the road to the west of the city and entered the Gennath Gate which led us to the western wall. There were workers and material everywhere.

King Herod began rebuilding the temple. Many believed as a monument to himself.

Supply carts cramped the streets.

Cursing and shouts and complaints filled the air.

We moved as quickly as we could.

The way to the Sheep Gate was completely blocked and we turned south.

Carts and donkeys were tied up in a compound that faced
south before the Central Valley.
I gave a boy a coin to keep watch. He was thrilled.

Mary had Yeshua bundled up and I went to retrieve the doves.
The little cage was empty.
We looked at Yeshua.
He had somehow pulled a rung loose
and that was that.
Our sacrifice had flown the coop.

"There's our answer, Mary." She took Yeshua in both hands
and held him high over her head to his delight. "So, you
weren't satisfied with these turtledoves, my little man?"
We climbed the temple steps that led through the main en-
trance to the Royal Porch.
I took Yeshua. Mary took my arm.
The steep steps were difficult for her.
Everything was polished and sparkling in preparation for
Passover week.
We decided it had all been done for Yeshua.
He didn't disagree.

There were soaring scaffolds along the south wall of the
temple itself and massive blocks stacked high. We walked
along Solomon's Portico with its colossal Corinthian col-
umns, and right through the Court of Gentiles.

The Dedication

Merchants' tables and stalls were prepared for the crowds to buy sacrifices or souvenirs.

Yeshua took in everything. He pulled my coat, leaned back over my arm, and hung his head on my shoulder.

The entire south face of the temple was under construction but we could enter the Court of Women through the Gate Beautiful.

The view was unobscured into the Court of Men through to the dazzling, gilded temple doors.

Marble gleamed. Polished and ready for a king.

The cauldrons stood on each side of the huge sacrificial altars.

They would soon be lit and burn for six nights and five days with the fat, flesh, and skins of thousands of lambs.

The drainage troughs waited for gallons of blood that would drain out of the Horse Gate into the Kidron.

"Joseph, our sacrifice."

We had forgotten.

"My name is Simeon. May I serve you?"

A pleasant looking old man—abrupt—with an odd, surprising question.

His tallith worn and faded, but not a tassel out of place. He had a few followers, and was apparently a temple priest.

I expected to be ushered to the Court of the Men for dedication when Simeon reached and took Yeshua from me with great joy before I thought to stop him.

He held him up, turned in a complete circle, and said in a
  loud voice,
> "Sovereign Lord, as you have promised,
> you now dismiss your servant in peace.
> For my eyes have seen your salvation,
> which you have prepared in the sight of all people,
> a light for revelation to the Gentiles
> and for glory to your people Israel."

Mary and I were amazed.
How could he know? How could anyone know?
What did he know? He said a revelation, a light for revela-
  tion to the Gentiles?
We are Jewish. Yeshua is Jewish. We are in the temple.

Then Simeon placed Yeshua in Mary's arms.
"Baruch atoi Adonai, Eloheinu melek ha olam." He spoke
  the blessing. "Blessed are you oh Lord our God, King of
  the Universe," and added 'blessed are your servants who
  serve you and this holy child.'"
Then Simeon turned and leaned in to Mary and spoke softly,
  "This child is destined to cause the falling and rising of
  many in Israel, and to be a sign that will be spoken against,
  so that the thoughts of many hearts will be revealed. And
  a sword will pierce your own soul."
Mary's face went white. Her eyes widened. She blinked back
  tears. Yeshua looked at her. Our Yeshua, who never cries
  had tears too.

"It's all right, my child. It's all right." Mary stroked Yeshua's cheek.

But we knew it wasn't.

We had been through many trials just to get to this moment, and I knew, this was a reminder. More would come.

"Anna, what do you want?" Simeon said to a woman who tugged his coat.

"Simeon, I want to see this child. Is he ...?" Anna looked ancient, stooped, stiff and slow. Harmless enough, but Mary was not going to give Yeshua to anyone except a priest. A temple priest.

"It's all right I tell you" Simeon rushed to tell us. "Anna is a prophetess, the daughter of Phanuel, of the tribe of Asher. She is a widow, and worships here night and day, fasting and praying."

"Thanksgiving to you, oh Lord my God, for this great thing," was all she said.

She was very respectful and Mary was not offended. But when Anna began scurrying around the grounds telling any who would listen, "Here is the redemption of Israel," many stared, frowned, then turned aside, shooing Anna away.

With that, Simeon turned us both and steered us to the entrance of the Court of Men. He ushered us along with urgency. Mary stopped short and handed Yeshua to me.

Simeon dragged me to the entrance of the temple grounds. Nine men waited with their baby boys for dedication.

Simeon pushed me up the steps to the entrance, right past the others, and then he stopped a young priest.

A very young priest, if you ask me.

"Yes, Simeon, so what is it?"

"Rabbi Nicodemus, here is the child to be dedicated. The one I have been waiting for. This is he." Simeon was pulling the priest's arm.

"All right, all right. So, bring me the boy." The rabbi stared at Yeshua.

"So, what is his name?" The other fathers were looking. They were not pleased that we were escorted to the front. Tongues clicked with grunts and grumbling. Simeon shushed them without sympathy.

"His name is Yeshua," I told the priest.

"The Lord is salvation. Amein, a name of promise. So, where is your sacrifice?" I could only think how embarrassing this is and wondered if I explained that …

"You there, bring me those two turtledoves. Be quick about it." Simeon shouted to one of his disciples, who dashed up the steps and handed the cage to the priest.

"So, this is your firstborn?" the priest asked.

"Yes."

"The mother is purified?"

"Forty one days today, Rabbi Nicodemus."

"He's a handsome boy, your Yeshua."

"You are kind. And you are right," I said, as if he needed my agreement.

"So, your tribe? What is your lineage?" The priest was in no hurry and the men behind were scuffing their feet and wagging their heads as their sons complained in the noonday sun.

"I am the son of Jacob from the house of David, the lineage of Abraham, our patriarch."

"I am familiar with the lineage of David. Do you know each generation?"

"Yes, of course. I am the son of Jacob, the son of Matthan, son of Eleazar, the son of Eliud, the son of ... "

"I believe you, Joseph. With your permission, may I release the doves?"

Simeon sighed, his eyes widened with his smile. The doves would not be killed or harmed in anyway. I had never heard of such a thing.

The priest pulled two rungs from the cage without waiting for an answer.

"I set you free and you will be free indeed," he said.

Then, listen to this, one of the turtledoves flew straight up and perched on the ledge over the grand doors to the temple. The other just stayed. I wondered if the dove was ill, an unacceptable sacrifice. I expected the priest to shake the cage and dump the dove, but at just that time it flew out and up and perched with the other.

Yeshua waved both arms and kicked both feet with a shriek of glee.

"Ahh, first Elijah and then the Savior," the priest said.

I wanted to leave immediately to tell Mary. Simeon squeezed
my arm.

"Apprentice," Nicodemus called without looking. "So, where
is my scroll?" A boy appeared and handed it to the priest.

"Blessed are you, our God Jehovah, King of the universe,"
the rabbi said as he unfurled the parchment rolled on two
spindles. He raised his head and his voice.
"From the second book of Torah;
'And it came to pass, when Pharaoh was stubborn
about letting us go,
that the Lord killed all the firstborn
in the land of Egypt,
both the firstborn of man and the firstborn of beast.
Therefore I sacrifice to the Lord
all males that open the womb;
but all the firstborn of my sons I redeem.'

"Bring me Isaiah." The boy rushed away, and another
came. I began to wonder how long we would be here.
Yeshua was completely calm.

The priest began again. He did not open this scroll. He simply
placed one hand on it, the other on Yeshua and began,
"Do not be afraid, O worm Jacob,
O little Israel,
for I myself will help you, declares the Lord,

112

> your Redeemer, the Holy One of Israel.
> See, I will make you into a threshing sledge,
> new and sharp, with many teeth.
> You will thresh the mountains and crush them,
> and reduce the hills to chaff.
> You will winnow them, the wind will pick them up,
> and a gale will blow them away.
> But you will rejoice in the Lord
> and glory in the Holy One of Israel."

He moved his hand to Yeshua's head. "You are dedicated to the Lord, Yeshua." He, Yeshua, looked at me. Then Rabbi said. "You are dedicated to Yeshua, Joseph."
And I felt justified with those words.
It was the truth, one that was long before the rabbi could imagine. Or could he? He just watched as we backed away. His hand poised in the air. He spoke something.
Mary was anxious to have Yeshua in her arms. I was in a fog. Simeon disappeared. Mary's eyes filled with tears when I told her about the doves as we started back to Bethlehem.

"Joseph, should we begin our journey home to Nazareth?" Mary said, holding the now sleeping Yeshua.
"Soon, but should we not raise the son of David in the City of David?"

SIXTEEN
Proud Papa

The next few months we discussed how long to stay.
  When to go home.
  What would be the next step in little Yeshua's life?
All the while wondering would his life be normal, or for
  how long?

We attended temple with Mary and Yeshua in the balcony.
To everyone's amazement, Hadad began to come.
We sent word home and explained as best we could why
  we were delayed so long.
As hard as I searched and tried, I could not find any property
  in my lineage in Bethlehem.
The census taker was of little help. An old centurion on his
  last duty, he said.

Work was steady and our savings became adequate for most
  emergencies.

Proud Papa

Our routine was set and I—we—considered that I would go
to Nazareth, collect a few things, and either close up our
house for a time or perhaps sell it. We were here in our
home away from home going on two years.

We honestly began to think our life would be plain
and perhaps predictable.
Yeshua was playing with the other children when not "helping" me arrange chunks of wood, shavings and chips.
His attraction to my work was what any father would want.
Yeshua could get as grimy as any of his friends, at least he
didn't mind being washed up, which Mary may need do,
two to three times a day.
His curly hair was hard to keep your hands out of and his
sparkling eyes melted your heart.
His quiet determination was a delight, but he spoke so little
we wondered if we were adequate parents.
"Mary, he speaks when he has something to say," I told her
mostly to reassure myself.
But it was true enough for now.
And, he went when he had somewhere to go.
Yeshua's laugh filled the house or yard, even temple.
The most joyous noise.
His hugs took your breath away.

"Yeshua, we don't need frogs in the house.
What have you done now? Are you bleeding again?"

was the daily chant from his mother.

He hated to disappoint her and didn't mind interrupting me.
　　He insisted on helping with any deliveries.

He was curious about everything, but for me, Yeshua in
　　temple was altogether a wonder. Though we received
　　condemning looks when Yeshua joined us at just a year
　　old, we had no reservations.

　　　　He was well mannered.

It was a struggle at first. Not about going to temple,
　　He just seemed dissatisfied with the balcony.
　　He would lean forward in Mary's arms till she was forced
　　to be right up to the railing.

Women and children were not allowed on the main floor
and for the most part were ignored.

"Mary," I asked once, "please move round to your right, and
　　I will move to the left. I will be able to see you both."

I had to admit, it was oft-times more interesting to watch
　　Yeshua than to listen to Rabbi Hadoram.

One day,

almost by accident, I thought.

Yeshua tugged my hand before we separated to go into temple.

When I looked to see what he may want, he lifted his arms
　　for me to take him.

Without even thinking I lifted him, and he hugged my neck.

Proud Papa

When Mary went to take him, he tightened his grip which
    made me gasp a bit.
"Yeshua," we both said.
But he held on, closed his eyes, shook his head every so
    slightly and said, "Abba."
Well, you can imagine, I was thrilled.
    Mary looked annoyed.
Yeshua called me Father, Abba.
"See, Mary, he speaks when he has something to say." Her look
    told me she might have something to say, but she didn't.

Only a few men even noticed I had him with me.
I eased to the back wall and sat on a bench.
Yeshua stood immediately up on my lap, leaned back against
    my left shoulder. Then he took one end of my talithe, my
    prayer shawl, and pulled it up over his head and tucked
    his curly hair beneath.
He was quite content, and obviously right where he wanted
    to be.
He placed his right arm round my neck like we were old
    friends.
        I nearly forgot where we were.
This may not really be my flesh and blood,
but it didn't make any difference,
not now, not here.
        Not anymore.

Then, just to shake my world altogether, Rabbi Rhokhim
    began, "Blessed are you, oh God, King of the universe."
And Yeshua said, his mouth right at my left ear,
"Baruch atoi Adonai," the Hebrew blessing.
Of course every man on the floor said "Baruch atoi Adonai"
but this was a first for Yeshua that I knew of. I know he had
    heard it many times, but he said it perfectly.
No, he didn't talk much, as I mentioned, but his speech
    wasn't babble.
When he said "Baruch atoi Adonai," I froze,
    wondering if I really heard this. Now, I know, you are
    thinking this is just a proud papa talking, and that's cer-
    tainly true, but still, I mean it.
He sounded his age, yes, but he spoke clearly.

My eyes must have looked like they were ready to fall out of
    my face. My jaw was so opened it started to cramp.
I saw Mary and her brow was creased with a curious look,
but I couldn't explain, not from here.

When I looked at Yeshua, he was not at all surprised at what
    he did, at what he said.
He just leaned in a little closer and stroked my beard, then
    he tilted his head, resting it on my face.
I was in heaven.
I couldn't wait to tell Mary.

SEVENTEEN
The Visit

Hadad brought Yeshua his first driedle and always, nearly always, brought a fresh loaf from his wife's oven and his prized honey.

Yeshua bounced on Hadad's generous belly and tugged on his beard.

Yeshua called him "uncle" one day and you would have thought Hadad was next in line to be king.

Speaking of kings.

It was dinner time after a long day.

Mary was bathing Yeshua.

At nearly two years old, he didn't need much help, except behind his ears and his constantly dirty elbows. And forget about his fingernails and sawdust coated head.

When they came.

We heard the commotion and the neighbor children scream-
ing with amazement. A trumpet blew. I went to see. I
walked through the door and stepped into a foreign land.
"Mary, Yeshua come."
We stood watching a caravan—a caravan from another world
stopped in our neighborhood, in front of our cottage.
The elephant announced their arrival with another
blast from its trunk.
There were camels, with braided manes,
and studded saddles and
embroidered reins with tassels.
Just behind were beautifully covered wagons
with large wheels and swags of curtains
still lurching back and forth.
There were carts with oriental rugs rolled and stacked.
There were crates of food, fruits, berries,
nuts and pomegranates.
And men, royals I guessed, wearing heavy beautiful robes
and fancy shoes that curled back in front.

Yeshua shook my hand loose and ran to greet the servant
boys who were dashing here and there, fetching stools
and rugs and crates.
He wanted to help.
Mary held her mouth at the splendor we saw.
We sat trying to take it all in.
Then two of the servants unrolled a carpet leading to our door.

The Visit

The whole of Bethlehem had come to see.
    Who could blame them?
"Joseph, are they here for Yeshua?"
"Who else, Mary?"
"Will they take him?"
"Oh my word, I hadn't considered that." But now I had to.
    And I thought, finally, royalty for Yeshua.

Yeshua came running back to us and the royals followed. The
    servants handed out small, deep blue-colored sacks to
    everyone and candied dates to the children.
Yeshua took our hands and led us out to our courtyard.
The men were right behind with servants behind them, each
    lugging ornate jars, fancy baskets, and fat leather sacks.
Yeshua climbed to sit on my work table, and each of the
    majestics bowed as their servants placed the gifts on the
    table around a calm, smiling, knowing Yeshua.
As they rose, they all kissed his forehead and spoke a blessing.
    The eldest placed a ring from his finger in Yeshua's hand.
Mary and I stared in awe.
Then they spoke to each other in a strange tongue.

Now this again, you won't believe, but that's your problem.
    You must, like us, come to expect the unexpected from
    Yeshua.
He answered them in their language—it's the truth.
    They spun around. Dropped to their knees.

He, Yeshua, placed his hand on them, one by one, and said
something in their tongue. With the seriousness of a sage.
I don't know what he said, but they knew.
They rose. Each one bowed and touched Mary and then
me. They didn't speak—their faces told us they were
overwhelmed.
As they left, Yeshua stood on the table and jumped into my
arms. I lifted him to sit on my shoulders and had to stoop
to pass under the doorway.
We watched the entourage as they prepared to leave.
They were not taking him! This was a relief and a mystery
as was the treasure they left.
There was a heavy sack of gold. A large jar of incense and
a basket of crystallized myrrh. And there was another
revelation, another prophecy in our sight, the Psalmist,
my ancestor, David, recorded his vision three thousand
years ago.

> The kings of Tarshish and of distant shores
> will bring tribute to him;
> the kings of Sheba and Seba
> will present him gifts.
> All kings will bow down to him
> and all nations will serve him.

The Visit

Temple was crowded on Shabbat.
The men made way as Yeshua and I entered.
Mary was treated with dignity and now *we* felt like royalty.
When it was time for the offering, our tithe was significant
    and murmurs echoed.
I tried to ignore all the fuss.

"Joseph, perhaps we should go back home now. I miss my
    family and friends, our precious little house."
"But, Mary, what if God sends more surprises for us right
    here?"

Our recent visitors were more than we could imagine.
I had to consider there might be more on the way to see us.
    To bring us things.
        That is, for Yeshua.

"Mary, we should just pray that God will give us clear direc-
    tion." And that was our heart of hearts.
    Of course I was thinking something simple.
Nothing like this.
    Who could think of anything like this?

EIGHTEEN
The Flight

It was a wonderful day of rejoicing.
Our Shabbat dinner was a feast.
Many neighbors,
    actually all of them, came for a visit to gape at our treasure.

I had to wonder why God would shower us with so much
    wealth.
Even the jars themselves were worth a small fortune.
Who would need so much in this little town of Bethlehem?

I slept on the roof that night after prayers of thanksgiving.
I looked toward the city from the little balcony, fully prepared
    to spend our life here.
    Oil lamps flickered in windows.
    Lazy smoke rose from campfires.
    A dog complained somewhere near Hadad's.
    I was overwhelmed with peace and drifted off.
        Until ...

"Joseph."

My mind awoke, but my body was asleep. I quickly felt his presence. The angel had returned. More good news I was confident.

"Joseph."

I wanted, tried to answer, but it was useless.

"Get up."

Now I really wanted to move ... but couldn't.

"Take the child and his mother and escape to Egypt. Stay there until I tell you, for Herod is going to search for the child to kill him."

Now I was fully awake and full of fear.

My child, my Mary in danger.

Why in the world would God place us in such danger?

I was angry.

I tore down the steps to wake Mary and Yeshua.

"What is it, my husband?" She was sitting straight up in bed.

"Mary, we have no time—none—pack quickly.

We are in danger. They want to kill Yeshua.

Us too no doubt."

"What are you saying? Who would ... " Mary's face went white.

"Please hurry. I'll explain later."

Yeshua was dressed.

Somehow I wasn't surprised.

I saw he'd been crying.

How could he know?
We had too much for just our donkey.
"Mary, I will leave some money for Jared for next month's
    rent and his cart."
"Whatever you say."
    The packing was frantic.
I had no idea how much time we had.

There sat two benches Ira asked me to build.
    Thank God they were finished.
        Now they were a gift.
        I didn't need the money.
And there is the stack of wood for Hadad.
        A tribute to him I never finished.
        I left the wood with a note of gratitude.

"Joseph, we are going home at last."
"Not yet, Mary. We are going to ... Egypt."
"Egypt? What will it be like for Jews in Egypt?"
"The angel said Egypt,"
    was all the answer I had.
        But she asked a good question.
From all I heard of Egypt we had no idea what to expect.
What would we find there?
How long?
Will we be in hiding?
Praise God we have funds.
More than enough.

The Flight

Looking back at Yeshua in the cart I saw he held a piece of
    bread in a cloth. I recognized the cloth from our wedding.
    That piece of bread had to be the matzo Rabbi Mattaniah
    told Mary, "Save for Messiah, surely to come." The matzo
    was two years old and yet perfectly fresh. A small piece of
    bread. An enormous reminder. Yeshua decided it would
    be his breakfast.

Looking back at the city I could only say,
    "Thank you, Bethlehem, for your kindness."
Looking back on our short life together
    I could only think, *what next?*
Questions filled my thoughts.
Fear gripped my heart.
Darkness surrounded me.
The evil one was after Yeshua.

I felt a battle raging all around me,
    through me,
    tearing at my mind.
    My legs felt like logs.
I pulled our donkey along, straining to put some distance
    behind us, and the dreadful warning.

      Would it ever end?

For additional copies of Mac's novels
please contact your local book store.

Also available:

www.BarnesAndNoble.com
www.Amazon.com
www.OneWayBooks.com

Bookstores please contact
STL Distribution
(800) 289-2772
www.STL-Distribution.com

All proceeds from book sales go to
One Way Books, a non-profit corporation.

ONE WAY BOOKS

For more information and book signing dates:
www.OneWayBookS.org
www.BibleActor.com
(954) 680-9095